Double, Double, Nothing But Trouble

Janet McNulty

This is a work of fiction. Names, characters, places, and incidents within are the product of the author's imagination or are used fictitiously, and any resemblance to actual persons, living or dead, business establishments, events, or location is entirely coincidental. The publisher does not have any control over and does not assume any responsibility for author or third-party websites or their content.

Double, Double, Nothing But Trouble

Copyright © 2015 Janet McNulty
Cover Illustration by Robert Henry

ISBN-13: 978-1-941488-19-5
ISBN-10: 1941488196

For any who have found themselves having a horrible week.

Double, Double, Nothing But Trouble

Chapter 1

Home. The thought of curling up in my own bed warmed me as Greg drove into the apartment complex parking lot and its cars that looked more like tombstones underneath the pools of light from the streetlamps. I tried to stifle a yawn, but Greg had noticed it and smiled.

"Tired?"

"A little," I replied, still yawning.

"Well, we're home. You can snuggle in your own bed tonight."

I grinned, pleased that we were back from Emily's Bed and Breakfast. Our romantic getaway had been anything but romantic, considering that I kept stumbling upon a dead body with a tendency to disappear the moment I tried to tell someone about it. After spending an entire day thinking I had gone crazy, and becoming a nuisance to those around me, the corpse showed up in Greg's and my bed. So long to romance. Our entire Valentine's Day weekend revolved around preventing a ghost named Billy from trying to exact his revenge on one of the employees because he thought that the man had killed him, while solving the mystery of his murder at the same time. Of course, there was one plus to the entire affair: Greg had proposed.

On the way back, we had decided to extend our get-away, stopping in a small town and skating on their out-door ice rink. We didn't return until late Monday night.

I glanced down at the engagement ring on my finger, admiring the way the tiny diamond glistened in the pale light. I was engaged. I repeated that sentence over and over in my mind, still not believing it.

Greg parked the car and turned off the engine. We both stepped out and grabbed our bags from the trunk, lugging them through the quiet parking lot and through the door to the stairwell that took us to the second floor. Being so late, I wasn't surprised that there was no one in the hallway and welcomed its emptiness, filled only by the lights that lined the top of the wall where the ceiling met it.

"Here, let me help you with that," said Greg, grabbing my suitcase as I tried to get my apartment key out to un-lock the door. I didn't want to wake Jackie by knocking.

I turned the key and opened the door, stepping into the dark interior of my apartment, giving Greg a kiss. Before

I had a chance to get all the way inside, the lights burst on and I found myself overwhelmed with shouts of "Surprise!"

So, Jackie hadn't been asleep after all. Within moments, Greg and I found ourselves pulled into my apartment surround by our friends laughing and clapping us on the back with congratulatory glee.

"Mel!" yelled Jackie as she hugged me and snatched my left hand, holding it, and the ring that was displayed with pride, into the light for all to see. "I knew he would! I'm so happy for you!"

She gave me another hug that almost squeezed the air from my lungs.

"How did you…" I began, but stopped. There was only one answer to my question: Rachel. I glanced around the room and found her standing in a corner away from everyone with a guilty expression on her face.

"I might have, kind of, let it slip," she said, but only I heard her. "I'll get those!" She sprang from the corner and seized my suitcase while I watched as it moved on its own to my bedroom.

"Hey, Mel!" Tiny walked up to me and swept me up in his huge, muscular arms in a giant bear-hug before slapping Greg on the back, causing him to stumble forward a bit from the impact. "I was wondering when you two would finally get engaged." He coughed a little as he said that.

"Are you feeling well?" I asked him.

"Just a little cold." He wiped his nose with a rag and sniffled loud enough to force any near him to take a step backward.

"Rachel told me the moment he proposed," said Jackie, handing Tiny a box of tissues as he continued to struggle with his runny nose. "So, I thought maybe a small party was in order."

"Thanks, Jackie," I said, stifling another yawn.

"I want to hear all about your romantic getaway," said Jackie.

"Uh…" I began.

"Well?"

"Maybe I should tell you later."

"Why?" Jackie gave me an accusatory look. "Don't tell me that you got involved in murder again."

"SHHH," I hissed at her. "Keep your voice down." I looked around at the others in the room, but they were too busy talking, eating, and drinking to have cared about Jackie's outburst. "Unfortunately, yes, but I will tell you later, once everyone leaves."

"I want all the details," said Jackie. "I swear, only you could get involved in murder when you're supposed to be on vacation."

She had a point. I did seem to get involved in a murder case at every turn. "I swear. I'll tell you later," I whispered to her.

"You better," she mouthed back.

I had to hand it to Jackie; she had planned the party out to every detail. Bags of chips, open dip containers, popcorn, smoked sausages, BBQ takeout (brought by Tiny I'm sure), two liter bottles of fizzing soda, and a single, untouched vegetable tray lined our kitchen counter. As I watched people eat, I forgot about my tiredness and listened to my stomach's nudge about feeding it, even though I wasn't hungry.

For the next several hours, I mingled and talked with those at that party, allowing guests to admire my engagement ring. Only one person remained absent: Rachel. Putting down my glass of untouched soda, I looked for Rachel and found her in my bedroom, staring out the window with a somber expression.

"Rachel?" I said.

"You should be at your party," she replied, still looking out the window, her opaque form fading in and out.

"But you're not there," I said. "I thought that you might be."

"I meant to, but…" her voice trailed off and at that moment I understood her solemn demeanor.

When I had first met Rachel, it was after Jackie and I moved into the apartment, which had been hers before she died. Rachel had been murdered, but before she was killed, she had gotten engaged to her long-time boyfriend, Tom. They had planned on getting married right after they both had graduated, but fate had other plans. I had helped her solve her murder, but in everything that had happened since, I never once considered finding her fiancé and helping her find closure for that area of her life. I had a feeling that even Rachel hadn't thought about it until now, until my engagement to Greg.

"Perhaps I should send everyone home," I suggested.

"No," said Rachel, "this is your moment. It's just… I'm afraid that in the afterlife you tend to forget about these moments, and I don't know why, but for some reason, I can't stop thinking about him."

"I think this has something to do with it." I held up my ring finger.

"I'll be fine," said Rachel. "Go and enjoy your party. That should be for the living anyway."

Knowing that nothing I said would ease her sense of sadness, I left, closing the door to my room to give her some privacy, and vowing to do something for her. It was time I had tracked down Tom so that Rachel could have some sense of closure.

Chapter 2

Tuesday morning arrived with bright sunshine, that glared off the snow, which had fallen the night before, with my alarm clock blaring and me not wanting to get up. Now that the weekend was over, it was time for me to get back to the grindstone. I rolled over and slapped my hand on my alarm clock to shut it up. All I ended up doing was knocking it to the floor, which forced me to crawl out of bed, pick it up, and turn it off. Well, mission accomplished. I was up.

I snatched my towel and ran to the bathroom, running right into Jackie.

"Whoa!" she said when she saw the mangled rat's nest that served as my hair. I ignored her exclamations and took a quick shower.

As I entered the kitchen (which still remained a mess from the half-eaten bags of chips, tipped over bottles of soda, and spoiled dip that never made it to the refrigerator), trying to unravel my hair with a comb, Jackie handed me a steaming cup of coffee.

"So," she said, "you were going to tell me about your romantic weekend and how it wasn't so romantic."

"A dead body showed up in our bed," I said, causing Jackie to spit her mouthful of coffee out.

"Only you, Mel," she said. "I swear, only you would get involved in a murder when you are supposed to be relaxing!"

"It's not like I wanted to. It's just… well, the ghost put his body there and then insisted that he knew who the murderer was, even though he never saw the person's face. Instead, he just convinced himself that one of the employees had done it and spent the whole weekend trying to exact some sort of revenge. I had to work double time just to keep him from committing a murder himself."

"So, you and Greg found out who did it?" Jackie leaned in, ready to hear more.

"Yes," I replied, "it was a couple who was there. They were looking for a partner of theirs, who had stolen a ruby from them, and killed Billy by accident."

"Billy?"

"The ghost."

I looked at my watch and gulped the rest of my coffee. "I'm going to be late!"

"Not a great impression for opening the store for the first time on your own," joked Jackie.

"See you at work," I said and ran out the door. Halfway

down the hall, I realized that I had forgotten the store key and charged back to my apartment where Jackie stood in the doorway, holding the key out to me, chuckling.

"You sure you got your car keys?" she called out to me.

"Yes!" I yelled back.

I parked my car on the street when I reached the strip that the Candle Shopped was on and fed the meter a bunch of quarters, hoping that it would buy me enough time until lunch, when I could escape and feed it some more. I was supposed to have been at work by 8AM, my first time opening the store. Mr. Stilton was the one who usually opened the Candle Shoppe, but last week he had decided that it was time to delegate some of his responsibilities. I think he just wanted to sleep in, in the mornings. Coming in early didn't bother me, other than the fact I was running late, because I needed the extra hours and the extra money.

I shoved the key (which opened both the front and back doors) into the lock of the entrance door and turned it, but it moved too easily. Undeterred by my misgivings, I opened the door and stopped. It looked as though a tornado had gone through there! What had once been pristine, porcelain warmers displayed in neat rows on shelves lay in a heap of broken shards on the linoleum floor. The few magazines we had, catering to people who loved candle making, littered the floor, ripped and torn with globs of melted slush and mud on them. I tiptoed over candles that laid on their side and rolled the moment my foot touched them, trying not to step on the broken warmers and bottles of oil—pools of the slick liquid threatened to trip me whenever I placed my foot down—so as not to crush the glass any further. My fingers found a switch and I flipped on the fluorescent lights, which made the store look like a disaster area, resembling the aftermath of hurricane Katrina more than a quaint candle shop.

Great, I thought to myself. Just great. I had just gotten back from a vacation that involved chasing after a vengeful ghost and returned home to find my place of employment ransacked. My eyes fell on the cash register. The safe! I ran to the backroom and opened Mr. Stilton's office, heading straight to the far corner where he kept the safe, and any money that had not been deposited yet. I knew the register would be empty. It was emptied every night after closing, but sometimes Mr. Stilton stayed late to work on inventory and was unable to get to the bank before it closed. So, he would place the undeposited finds in his safe.

I turned on the light and stopped when I noticed the safe. It was untouched. I examined it closer, looking for any signs of it having been tampered with, but it appeared that whomever had broken into the store had not been interested in the money. That was strange. Weren't most break-ins a result of the thief looking for money, or something of great value that they could sell? I turned and saw a massive hole in the wall. Why would the thief be knocking holes in the wall? Was he angry about something?

Pulling myself from my natural tendency to start trying to solve a mystery, I yanked my phone from my pocket and started looking up the number for the local police station, before remembering that I had Detective Shorts' number programed. Over a year ago, I had gotten into trouble, solving another murder of course, and lost my phone. In an effort to keep my sleuthing under control, Detective Shorts had bought me a new cell phone with his number programed on speed dial.

"Miss Summers?" came his curt, businesslike voice on the other end.

Why was I not surprised that he had my cell number programmed on his phone as well? "Detective," I replied, "I need you to come down to the Candle Shoppe right away."

"Is something wrong?" His voice changed from all-business to concern.

"I was opening up today and the entire place has been ransacked."

"I'm on my way. Do not go inside."

Too late.

"You're inside, aren't you?"

"Yes," I replied.

"I want you to go outside, right now, and wait for me. I mean it. And don't touch anything."

He hung up and I put my phone back in my pocket. I didn't go outside right away. The hole in the office wall seemed odd and begged for my attention. I poked my head in and looked to my left and my right, trying to make out what I could in the darkness, but there was nothing of interest and despite a few bits of insulation, the wall was hollow. I wish I had my flashlight with me, then I could see inside it better.

My phone buzzed. "Hello?" I answered it.

"Miss Summers, I'm standing just outside the entrance to the store, but you're nowhere to be found."

Darn it! I allowed my curiosity to get the better of me again and forgot to make sure that I was outside before the detective arrived. Before doing anything else, I sent a quick text to both Jackie and Greg, letting them know what had happened and not to worry; I was fine. My phone buzzed again with Detective Shorts' number on the caller ID. I hurried out of Mr. Stilton's office, through the house of horrors that now made up the shop, and out the door, running right into Detective Shorts.

"Miss Summers," he said, the annoyed tone in his voice evident, "when I tell you to wait for me outside, I mean for you to wait for me—*Outside*!"

"Yes, detective," I said. "I was just… well… there was…" Oh what's the use? The man knew me too well and nothing I said would convince him that I was not snooping.

Detective Shorts motioned for the officers who were with him to go inside. Their heavy boots crunched what was left of the ceramic warmers while the lights from their cameras flashed at repeated intervals from the pictures they took.

"You were here alone?" asked the detective, his notepad and pen out, ready to take my statement.

"Yes," I replied, "I was opening the store this morning and saw all of this." I waved my hand at the mess.

"Did you see anyone as you came in?"

"No."

"Did you touch anything?"

"Yes. I went into the back office and checked the safe."

"Was anything missing from it?"

"It's still there and it's still locked. It doesn't appear to have been tampered with."

"And the cash register?"

"Empty. It's emptied every night before closing and the money is either put in the safe or deposited at the bank."

"Did you touch anything else?"

"No," I said, but my innocent tone betrayed me.

"Miss Summers?"

"I didn't touch it. There is this hole in the back wall. I never touched it! I just… looked through it."

Detective Shorts glowered at me. "Can you think of anyone who might want to break in here?"

"No," I replied. "We just sell candles. Nothing worth stealing and we never have that much cash in the register. Most people pay with debit cards these days." I pointed at the sign in the store window with the familiar logos of credit card institutions and that read, "We take all major cards". Mr. Stilton had finally decided to upgrade to the 21st century and start accepting credit/debit cards. It was easier than dealing with the amount of bad checks that some people wrote.

Movement caught my eye. I turned my head and saw a man, he stood in the shadows and seemed to be unaware of the commotion around him, loitering in a corner. He looked familiar, but I couldn't be sure.

"Miss Summers?"

"What?" I snapped back to the present and remembered why I was here. When I looked back to where the man had been, no one was there.

"What happened?" Mr. Stilton ran up to us in a huff, his big, disbelieving eyes darting from one police officer to the next as he gawked at the scene. Poor man. I was just an employee here. I'm not sure what I would have done if it had been my business that had been broken into.

"Mr. Stilton," said Detective Shorts, trying to calm the man down, "my name is Detective Shorts. You're store is the scene of a possible robbery."

"No kidding!" shouted Mr. Stilton.

"I need you to go through here and make a list of anything that is missing. Miss Summers says that the safe is intact, but I would like you to do your own assessment. One of my officers will accompany you."

Still in a state of shock, Mr. Stilton just nodded and allowed himself to be led away, while the officer made notes of anything he said.

My phone buzzed again. It was a text from Greg. *Are you okay? I'm coming over.*

I texted him back, telling him that I was fine and there was no need since I was busy speaking to the detective.

Another text arrived. *Are you sure? I can take time off from work.*

Smiling, I replied that, yes, I was sure and that I would see him later. Before I had a chance to put my phone back in my pocket, it buzzed for the fifth time that morning, this time, from Jackie.

Mel! OMG! You okay?!

Ignoring the others round me, I texted her back, telling her that I was surrounded but a bunch of cops, so she needn't worry. After I put my phone back in my pocket, I looked up to find Detective Shorts staring at me with an annoyed look on his face.

"Do you think you can put a cork in your social life for a moment to concentrate on this?" he asked.

"Sorry," I mumbled.

My phone rang. It was Greg. Before I could answer it, Detective Shorts snatched my phone and put it up to his ear. "Miss Summers is busy right the moment and will have to call you back. And unless you want to be arrested for getting on my nerves, I suggest you quit interrupting my investigation."

He handed my phone back to me and I took it, looking mortified. Poor Greg! I could just imagine what he was thinking.

"I need you to walk me through everything that you did after arriving here this morning," said the detective.

I just nodded my head in response.

For the next hour, Detective Shorts followed me as I explained how I had arrived, unlocked the door, found the place a mess, and went to the back room. He frowned when I demonstrated how I poked my head through the hole in the wall while trying to not touch it. We were on our way back out when…

"Ma'am!" shouted Detective Shorts, running up to a woman (mid-30s I guessed), trying to enter the Candle Shoppe. "You need to step away from here right now."

"Oh, I'm sorry," said the woman.

"What are you doing here?" demanded Detective Shorts.

"Nothing. I… This place is usually open by now and I was hoping to get a gift for my aunt."

"Did you not notice all of the officers here and the broken glass?" asked Detective Shorts, his arms crossed in that doubtful pose of his.

"I did," replied the woman, "but I'm afraid I got a little curious and just forgot myself."

"I need you to leave." Detective Shorts waved an officer over to escort the lady away. "This is an active crime scene. You're lucky I don't have you arrested for obstruction."

"Oh, I would never…" began the woman.

Detective Shorts got a thoughtful look on his face, almost as though he recognized her, but couldn't place where he had seen her before. "Do I know you?"

"I don't see how," said the woman. "We've never met."

"You look familiar."

"I'm sure I just got one of those faces," said the woman.

"Perhaps," Detective Shorts replied. He motioned for an officer to escort her away, while I just stood there trying to figure out their little exchange. I had never seen her before, but that didn't mean much—this was a city—and he sees so many people each day because of his work, that she must just look familiar.

"Miss Summers," he said, "I believe we are done here, unless there is something else you can think of."

"Sorry," I replied, "no."

"You can go home then, but I want you to remain available in case I have any more questions."

"Thanks, detective," I said.

I walked down the sidewalk, not sure what to do or where to go. I didn't want to leave anyway because I wanted to know who would break into a candle store. I stopped in front of the flower boutique. With everything that had happened, I had forgotten about Rachel and a thought occurred to me: where was she? When trouble happened, and if Rachel was nearby, she was the first to show up. So, why wasn't she here now?

As I stood on the sidewalk, I saw the same man again, except… Was he inside the flower shop? How'd he get in there? As I stared at him, I realized where I had seen him before. Ever since the first day I had started working at the Candle Shoppe, I had seen this man and pegged him as one of those customers that regularly stop in small stores and look around. If he worked at the flower boutique, which was next door to where I worked, then that would explain why he was always around. I'm afraid I do not know the people who work at the little shops near the Candle Shoppe, but I was never as good at making friends like Jackie was. I started to head over to him, but a voice stopped me.

"Do they know anything?"

I turned. It was the same woman that had tried to walk into the Candle Shoppe earlier. "I don't think I'm supposed to talk about it."

"No, I understand," said the woman. "I was just hoping…" She shuddered, and not from the cold.

"Are you all right?" I asked.

"It's just a little scary. You know?" said the woman. "Having a place I shop at robbed."

"A little," I said, though I didn't feel that freaked out about it, considering that I tend to attract trouble the way honey attracts ants.

"Aren't you scared?"

"Not really," I said. "Trouble tends to find me, so let's just say that I'm used to it."

"Not me."

I was about to leave, but the woman just stood there, looking like she might have an emotional breakdown; so, I stayed. "Do you want to go get some coffee? There's a place right over there."

"Sure."

We walked across the street to a café, welcoming the warmth that wafted over us, sending the chill that seized our skin away, as we stepped inside. There wasn't much of a line, sort of a misnomer, allowing us to get our coffees and find a place to sit.

"You never did tell me your name," I said.

"Jillian. Jillian Modsen." Her black curls brushed the dark skin of her cheeks as she sipped her coffee.

"Mellow Summers, but everyone just calls me Mel, except for my aunt who is a bit on the insane side."

"She'd make a room full of nuts look sane," said Rachel, answering the question of where she was. "God bless her certifiably insane soul, but I'm kind of glad she's not around."

I smiled at her, but tried to pretend I was smiling at Jillian. It wouldn't be a good idea to let her think I was crazy.

"So, I heard this little rumor," continued Rachel, but only I heard her, "that your place of employment has been robbed. And you didn't call me!"

"It's not like you have a cell phone," I whispered out of the side of my mouth to her.

"What?" said Jillian.

"Nothing," I replied, taking another sip of my coffee.

"Yeah," said Rachel to me, "that might have something to do with it. So, come on! What are you sitting here for? We need to investigate!"

I looked at Jillian, hoping that Rachel would understand my dilemma.

"What, her? You worry too much," said Rachel.

"Oh," said Jillian, "now I know why your name is familiar. You're that psychic, or whatever."

"Or whatever?" Rachel put her ethereal hands on her hips. "I'll have you know…"

"I don't really think of myself as a psychic," I said, cutting Rachel off.

"Well, the word around town is that you can speak to spirits and have even been very instrumental in helping the local PD solve certain cases."

"I can't really talk about all of that," I said.

"Though, I'm not sure if I believe in all of this ghost nonsense," said Jillian.

"Nonsense!" roared Rachel, causing a few heads to turn in our direction.

"I mean, I have a friend who is into to all of that stuff," continued Jillian, "but I am a bit skeptical. Not trying to insult you or anything, but let's face it, there are a lot of fakes out there."

"Do you believe in me now, huh?" Rachel kicked the legs of Jillian's chair.

"Sorry," I said. "I tend to forget that these tables are so small."

"Hey, where's my donut?" demanded one grumpy customer at the counter; his rolls of belly fat pushed against his already strained belt.

"You don't need it pork-butt!" shouted Rachel, allowing the entire café to hear her.

I put my head in my hands.

"Are you okay?" asked Jillian.

"Just a little tired," I said. "So, why are you telling me all of this about your friend? Did you agree to come with me here just to belittle me?"

"No! Sorry. I tend to be skeptical by nature, but my friend just lost someone close to her and… well… I was wondering if you'd like to…"

"We will," Rachel answered for me and Jillian heard her, but mistook her statement as my answer.

Great. So, now I have a séance to perform. I glared at Rachel. What was she trying to do? Get me into even more trouble?

"Great! Um… six o'clock tonight?" said Jillian.

"Sure," I replied, knowing that since Rachel had committed me to it, there was no getting out of it.

"About that candle store today," said Jillian, "with your sleuthing reputation, are you going to just let the police handle it? I know I wouldn't if it was where I worked."

"I should say not!" said Rachel, remembering to keep her voice where only I heard her.

"For now, I think it's best to let the police do their job," I said.

"I can't believe what I'm hearing," Rachel said to me.

"Excuse me," I said, "I need to get some napkins."

I scooted my chair back and walked over to the napkin display, hoping that Rachel would get the message and follow me, which she did.

"What are you doing?" I whispered to her.

"Your work gets robbed and you're just sitting here, sipping away on your coffee like nothing's happened," Rachel replied.

"Somehow, I don't think that is why you are really upset."

"Miss African-American over there doesn't believe in ghosts. In me!" Rachel turned towards Jillian. "I'm right over here you dingbat!"

I shushed Rachel. We didn't need a scene.

"Come on," said Rachel, tugging on my arm, "let's go to the Candle Shoppe."

"I can't."

"Why not?"

"The police are probably still there. My poking around will attract attention. You, on the other hand, can go unnoticed."

"Are you trying to get rid of me?" teased Rachel.

"Maybe," I said. "Look, I know Detective Shorts. He'll be expecting me to show back up, but he won't be looking for you."

"Okay, then, you have a deal," said Rachel, shaking my hand and causing my triceps to jiggle. "And don't even think about skipping out on that séance tonight. I know where you live. I'm so looking forward to it!"

Rachel sauntered through the coffee shop, bumping into Jillian's chair as she passed and causing her to spill her coffee. I just shook my head and went back to my seat with a handful of napkins, which I used to clean up the spilt coffee.

"I'm not so sure about this séance tonight," I said. "I don't normally do such things."

"Oh, please come," urged Jillian. "It will make my friend happy."

I nodded in agreement.

"Here"—Jillian handed me a slip of paper with an address on it—"this is where she lives."

"All right," I said, taking the paper, and knowing that Rachel would never let me get out of this anyway. "I should go."

"No worries! I'll see you tonight."

Smiling at her, I picked up my coffee and left the café, glancing at the address she had given me. Since I wasn't familiar with its location, I pulled out my cell phone and looked it up on the internet. It wasn't far from where I lived. I put my phone away, hoping that Rachel had a plan.

Chapter 3

I stood on the sidewalk leading up to a quaint, single-story, ranch home in the last rays of the late afternoon sun. There didn't seem to be any life in the house. It was quiet. Too quiet for my taste. I checked the slip of paper which Jillian had given me in the coffee shop. Yep. the address matched.

Deciding to get this over with, and knowing that Rachel would never let me get out of this since she volunteered me, I shoved the slip of paper in my jeans pocket and walked up to the pale blue door with a wreath, smothered in red hearts and flowers, hanging from it. Whomever lived here hadn't taken down their Valentine's Day decoration, which came as no surprise, since Valentine's Day was only a few days ago.

I stepped up onto the porch, being careful to avoid the small patch of ice, and knocked. No answer. I knocked again. As I waited in the cold, wondering if Jillian had given me the wrong address, hurried footsteps echoed from inside and the door opened. A woman greeted me, but it wasn't Jillian.

"Hi," I said, "I'm Mellow Summers. Jillian asked me to come."

The woman's face brightened upon the mention of Jillian's name. "Yes, yes, come in! We've been expecting you."

She opened the door wider, allowing me inside. I tried to knock the snow off my boots as best I could, not wanting to track any in the house or on the floral rug that stretched down the length of the hallway.

"We're through here," said the woman, leading me down the hallway. "I'm so glad that you've agreed to come. I'm, Lily."

"Nice to meet you," I said.

Lily took me through the hallway with full of soft lighting and to a small den. The curtains had been drawn and a table was set up in its center, complete with a table cloth coated in stars and moons with a crystal ball sitting atop it, and three chairs.

"Uh… I can see you've been busy," I said.

"We thought that we ought to try and set up the proper atmosphere," replied Lily. "You can put your coat and purse over there."

I set down my things on the credenza that Lily had pointed me to. "Where's Jillian," I asked.

In answer to my question, Jillian waltzed in, in a

jovial manner, and a huge grin, beaming at me. "Mel! I'm glad you made it. I know this was all short notice."

"I don't normally do these sorts of things," I said. "I'm not into all of this showy stuff."

Where was Rachel? She was the one who had pushed me into this.

"I hope we got everything set up properly," said Jillian.

I looked at the table and its stars and moon table cloth. Really? Does everyone take what they know about séances from movies and television shows?

"It's a bit much. A basic table would have sufficed," I said, "and we don't really need that." I pointed at the crystal ball. "I never use one, " I added, in an attempt to not sound insulting. I was a guest, after all.

"Oh, leave it," said Rachel, sitting crossed-legged on the table. Thank God she showed up. This was her idea. I could tell by the way Lily and Jillian ignored her that only I saw and heard Rachel.

"Shall we get started?" asked Jillian with excitement.

I guess there was no time like the present. "Sure," I replied, taking a seat at the table. "I guess we ought to dim the lights."

Lily had beat me to it and darkened the room, before sitting next to Jillian.

"Okay," I said, trying to sound like I knew what I was doing, even though I was winging the entire thing, "first I need to know a bit about whom you are trying to contact."

"Well, his name is Ronald," said Lily. "He's my brother."

"Doubt it," snapped Rachel.

I glared at her.

"Oh, come on. Does she look like she knows a Ronald?"

"Are you sure that is your brother's name?" I asked.

Jillian got a surprised look on her face.

"You're right," said Lily. "Sorry, to trick you, but I wanted to be certain that you are the genuine article. I've been to fake psychics before."

"I'm not really psychic," I said.

Both Lily and Jillian passed off my objections as though I was being modest.

"My brother's name was really Doug," Lily said.

"Bingo!" Rachel blurted out, but only I heard her, holding up a photograph of a man that had a striking resemblance to Lily.

"What would you like me to do?" I asked.

"Well…" began Lily, "I'd like you to contact him. Um… I'd like to be able to speak with him. He died soon after we had an argument and I never got the chance to say I was sorry."

Lily's story made me want to cry. I felt for her. I know how much of a wreck I would be if Greg and I had an argument and he died before we had a chance to make up. I decided that the least I could do was try to contact her brother; and I had Rachel here to help me.

"I can't make any promises," I said. Some spirits don't mind mingling with the living—"

Rachel giggled at that statement.

"—and some prefer to be left alone."

Both Lily and Jillian, who seemed to be watching me with apt attention, nodded.

"We should hold hands." I had seen enough T.V. to

know that in many séances people held hands as a way of communing with the spirits. We each took one another's hands and I looked at Rachel, hoping that she would read my unspoken question: where is this Doug? Lucky for me, Rachel was a mind reader as well as a ghost. She disappeared.

"I wish to speak with the spirit named Doug who is the sister of this woman," I said, doing my best to make my voice sound authoritative, yet mystical at the same time. "Doug? Can you hear me, Doug?"

Nothing. I hoped Rachel would return soon.

"Do you have anything of his?" I asked Lily.

She shook her head.

"I am trying to contact the spirit known as Doug," I tried again, but had a feeling that I wasn't going to have much luck.

"Hey!" said Rachel as she popped into the room beside me, making me jump a little. "So, I searched and searched, but there is no spirit named Doug. At least, not one who is related to her." She pointed at Lily.

"What are you saying?" I whispered to her.

"Is he here?" asked Lily. She must have heard me.

"I'm saying that either she has no brother, or he isn't dead," replied Rachel.

"What?" I said, louder than I had planned. My heart sank as I realized that something wasn't right. "Can you do something?"

"Leave it to me," said Rachel.

"Are you getting anything," said Jillian, "because I do have other things to do."

Rachel motioned for me to say something. "There is a spirit here," I said, "but it's not Doug. Her name is... Rachel."

"But I wanted to speak with Doug," said Lily.

"Well he ain't here!" shouted Rachel and, judging by the surprised looks on their faces, I knew that both Lily and Jillian had heard her. Rachel motioned at me to say something again.

"She is very angry," I said. "She says that Doug is not dead, but alive. Living in..."

"West Virginia," Rachel finished for me.

Lily's face paled. Her ruse had been found out and she didn't like it.

"I think..." began Jillian, starting to stand up, but Rachel forced her back into her chair.

"And you," Rachel said so all could hear her, "you don't believe in ghosts, huh? Well, I am here. I've always been here you skeptical..."

"Rachel," I interrupted her, "do you have something you would like to tell us all?"

"Ghosts are real," said Rachel.

Jillian's face pinched in disbelief.

"Oh, so you don't believe me?" snapped Rachel. She jumped on the table and kicked the crystal ball off it, while at the same time the lights brightened and dimmed on their own. "Lights on! Lights off!" she kept saying each time the lamps flickered on and off. "OOOO—This is so much fun!"

Before I knew it, Rachel started dancing on the table, causing it to wobble back and forth. Lily screamed while Jillian's eyes turned wide, though they looked all around as though she still didn't believe what she saw and heard.

"Rachel," I said as she continued to do a jig on the table, scuffing its varnish. "Rachel!"

Rachel stopped and hunched her shoulders, giving me a pouty face.

"I think they get it," I said to her.

"Fine." She jumped off the table, making certain to give it a good shake as she did so. "I'll go." Rachel started for the door and paused, facing both Lily and Jillian, and materializing before them, while staying somewhat transparent for their benefit.

"I do exist!"

She vanished.

I released their hands. "I think that is enough for now."

"What was that?" demanded Jillian.

"An angry ghost," I said.

"Excuse me?"

"You wanted a séance," I reminded Jillian. "I told you that I don't do these sorts of things, but you got what you wanted."

"I didn't expect..." began Jillian.

"Doug isn't dead, is he?" I demanded.

"No," replied Lily in a soft whisper, her face guilt-ridden. "I... I think you should go."

I agreed with her, wondering what all of this had been about and snatched my coat and purse.

"Mel!" yelled Lily, chasing after me with Jillian right behind her as I hurried out the door, while struggling to get into my coat. The moment I stepped through, a glob of snow sailed through the air, striking Jillian in the face.

"Ha-ha! Got ya!" shouted Rachel with glee. "That'll teach you, you skeptic!"

I just stared at Rachel in disbelief. Jillian looked livid and Lily was in the same state of shock I was. Before either had a chance to say anything, I ran down the walk, skidding on a tiny patch of ice, and to my car. I got in, started the engine, and sped off, wishing that I hadn't let Rachel talk me into the séance and hoping that there wouldn't be any repercussions.

Chapter 4

"Mel?"

I ignored the distant voice that spoke my name. All I wanted to do was sleep.

"Mel?"

I opened one eye. Jackie's picture perfect, and worried, face filled it. Though still groggy, I lifted my head and opened my other eye. "What time is it?" I asked through a yawn.

"Seven in the morning," replied Jackie. "You have a class in two hours."

I sat up and my mind focused as I looked around. I was not in my room. When I got home last night, I must have sat on the couch and fallen asleep.

"Are you okay?" asked Jackie. "You look worried."

"I don't know," I said. "Rachel talked me into conducting a séance for someone who didn't believe in ghosts."

"What?" Jackie looked at me dumbfounded.

"Yeah… well… it didn't go well."

"Are you sure you're okay, though? I mean, after finding the store robbed and all."

"I'll be fine. It didn't look like anything was taken." I glanced at my watch and realized that if I was going to make my class on time, I needed to shower and change, especially since I had slept in my clothes from the day before.

"Mel!" Greg walked in and gave me a giant hug. "Are you sure you're all right after yesterday?"

"You know, you're the second person to ask her that," said Rachel, materializing before all of us.

Greg and Jackie no longer jumped when she appeared, having gotten used to her presence over the last couple of years.

"I'll be fine," I said, giving Greg a kiss. "Let me shower really quick and you can take me to my first class."

"Agreed," said Greg.

"You know what you can do, in the meantime," Rachel said to Greg, while I entered the bathroom, "make her some breakfast. Mel will take two eggs, over easy, some waffles with maple syrup, and a bowl of fruit. Chop! Chop! Get to it. She doesn't have all morning!"

I smiled at Rachel's antics. I admired Greg for tolerating her ordering him around, not that anyone could force her to stop. She was a free spirit, in more ways than one, and did as she pleased.

I hurried through the shower, threw on some fresh

clothes, including a button up blouse that Jackie had made me purchase last week, and ran into the kitchen where, to my surprise, was a bountiful breakfast, made by Greg. He stood next to the table, wearing Jackie's floral apron and I knew Rachel had made him put it on, with a plate full of waffles (the cook in the toaster kind), eggs (over easy), a small bowl of fresh cut fruit, and a steaming cup of coffee.

"Your breakfast awaits," said Greg, pulling out a chair for me to sit in.

"You didn't have to," I said.

"I'm pretty sure I did," said Greg.

Rachel appeared in the kitchen. "You got yourself a keeper there. That man can cook. Well… sort of." She glanced at the empty box of frozen waffles.

"And for your waffles." Greg handed me a container of warm syrup.

"Thanks," I said.

"Come on, eat up. We don't have all day."

I glared at Rachel.

"What? Sorry."

I dug into my waffles and eggs, saving the fruit for last. Once done, we cleaned up the dishes, and Jackie shooed Greg and me out the door. "I'll meet you at work later," she said. "Mr. Stilton wants us to come in and help clean up."

I nodded that I had heard her. As I rushed down the hall with Greg. We got in his car and were at the college in about ten minutes.

"Greg," I said, before getting out of the car. "Do you think Jack can find Rachel's old boyfriend?"

Greg eyed me, confused as to why I would ask such a thing.

"During our little surprise engagement party, Rachel seemed down and I think it was because she was remembering Tom. Remember, she had been engaged when she was murdered."

"Yeah, I remember," Greg replied.

When I had first moved to Vermont with Jackie, we found ourselves a nice little apartment that was already furnished for very little rent. We didn't know it at the time, but that apartment had been Rachel's before she died and she never left. Soon after, I found myself wound up in an unsolved murder case, hers in fact, and that was the start of my career as a sleuth, not that I ever got paid for it.

"I think we should try to find him for her, so that she can have some closure," I said.

"What was his name."

"All I have is a first name: Tom."

"I'll call Jack and have him dig into it. I can't make any promises, though. Now, you better get going, or you'll be late."

"I'll see you later," I said to Greg as I kissed him and jumped out of the car.

I watched him leave to head for work. He only had to attend class one day a week, as most of his courses were online this semester. I started to think that perhaps I should look into doing that, but not all of my courses were offered online. Checking my watch, I realized that I had about fifteen minutes until my class started, so I headed to the Student Union to get something to drink from their cafeteria.

As I hiked across the campus, I noticed a few people staring at me. I watched them as they pointed and talked in hushed whispers, their feeble attempt to disguise the fact that they were talking about me. Ignoring them, I picked up my pace to a brisk walk, welcoming the warmth of the Student Union as I stepped inside. Again, people stared at me, giving me odd and accusatory glances. What was their problem? Did I know them? Had I done something to offend them? I didn't remember ever seeing them before, except maybe in passing. I brushed off their stares and hurried to the cafeteria. The aroma of cooking pancakes, sausage, hash browns, and brewed coffee filled my nostrils the moment I entered the bustling area and its sounds of dinnerware and clinking forks.

I spotted the hot beverage section and went over there, picking up a small Styrofoam cup. Coffee or hot chocolate? I settled on hot chocolate, since I had already had at least one cup of coffee. Besides, I have a weakness for chocolate. As I filled my cup, I knocked over one that was half-filled, which someone had abandoned on the counter, spilling its contents all over the table with some of it dripping onto the scuffed floor. The brown liquid sloshed over the edge of the counter, covering a newspaper that someone had left on a tiny stand. I snatched a wad of napkins and tried to clean up the spilt drink, but stopped when I noticed that my face was plastered on the front page of the local newspaper. I picked it up, doing my best not to tear the soaked page.

Mediums: Fraud or Genuine?

Jillian Modsen

The world has its fair share of those claiming to be psychics or mediums. You know the story: someone claiming to be able to speak with the spirit of those who have died, and people so desperate to believe it and reconnect with loved ones, that they fall for it. It appears that psychics are everywhere. We even have our very own.

Her name is Mellow Summers, or Mel, as she is known to her friends. She claims that she not only can speak to ghosts, but sees them as well. She refuses to go into any detail about how this all started, but it is rumored that she has used her abilities to assist the local police in solving certain cases, including the case of a murdered college student that went unsolved for an entire year.

Being a natural skeptic myself, I decided to invite Miss Summers over for a séance, so that I could see the action for myself. I must admit that she did not disappoint in giving my friend and me a show; and I am curious as to how she managed to make it look like an actual spirit had appeared. Amidst the rapping table, flickering lights, and disembodied voice—ventriloquism must be one of Miss Summers' many talents as there is no other way she could have pulled it off—we were quite entertained. Though my friend is somewhat convinced about her otherworld abilities, I am not.

We had decided to see if our self-proclaimed psychic could contact my friend's deceased brother. Mellow wasted no time in informing us that we were putting her on. Fair enough. But as I explained to my friend, she could have easily spotted the birthday card that had arrived in the mail that day and was on the front table as she walked in.

But the question remains: if Mellow Summers is a true psychic, then why is it she failed to foresee that the Candle Shoppe, the very place where she is employed, would be robbed. Yesterday morning, reports say that the police were there investigating a break-in discovered by—you guessed it—Miss Summers herself.

Some of you might say that such a gift doesn't work that way. Perhaps. But since Miss Summers has been essential in assisting the local police with several murder investigations over the last three years, I believe that the people have the right to know if her psychic ability is genuine, especially since it has been instrumental in sending certain individuals to the state penitentiary. For now, this juror is still out on her verdict.

Why that little… All sorts of curses and colorful words filled my mind as I thought about how she had used me and how I had fallen for it. I couldn't believe that I had been so dumb. I thought I had been comforting someone who was shaken up about the break-in and helping another find some sort of peace. I felt used and I did not like being taken advantage of. I smacked the paper on the counter, finished filling my cup of hot chocolate, took it to the cashier, and paid for it. She gave me a double take as though she had seen me before, which meant that she had probably seen my picture in the paper, but remembered herself.

"$2.99," she said.

I gave her three ones and told her to keep the penny. I shoved my way past a group of younger students, who all laughed and giggled when they recognized me, and rushed out the door, jogging to my class. As luck would have it, everyone seemed to have read the local paper that morning; their eyes followed me wherever I went.

I ran into the classroom and found a seat in the back, hoping that once the professor started speaking, the other students would quit passing glances in my direction.

"Hey, look. It's the psychic," said one.

I glowered at him. Were we back in high school all of the sudden. I thought we were supposed to be adults, but I guess some people never grow up.

"So, psychic," continued the same person, "what do you predict my future will be?"

"Leave me alone," I told him.

"What? You don't like all of the attention?"

I saw Rachel appear beside him with an irate expression on her face. "If you're not careful," I said, "you'll end up on the floor."

The person laughed as he sat on the edge of his seat, but at that moment, Rachel slammed her fist into him and knocked him to the floor. He landed on his back and looked around in shock, not comprehending what had happened.

"That's for making fun of my friend!" yelled Rachel.

"You pushed me somehow!" accused the man.

"How?" I asked. "I'm sitting over here."

The others in the room watched our exchange, just as confused as he was about his sudden face to face meeting with the carpet.

"I don't know, but you had…"

Rachel's eyes flared. "It was me!" She shoved him again. "I'm the one who pushed you. And I'll keep shoving you around until you leave Mel alone!"

I looked at Rachel, pleading with her to stop. Disappointed, she left the poor man alone—who remained standing, trying to figure out what had happened—and sat in a desk next to mine.

"I knew that lady was up to no good," she said, "especially after she said that she didn't believe in ghosts. No self-respecting person denies the existence of spirits." She folded her arms and slumped on the desk.

At that moment, the professor marched into the room and placed his armful of books on the front desk. He said nothing as he picked up a dry erase marker and wrote a set of instructions on the board. The others in the room quieted down, pulling out their tablets.

"See you later," said Rachel as she vanished.

This particular professor was a no-nonsense kind of man, who liked getting down to business. Every class period, he would walk into the classroom, write an assignment on the board, and we were to complete it before class had ended. Today's assignment consisted of downloading an audio file, which he had posted on his website, and manipulating it, using a piece of audio software that we had to purchase, to create something fresh and new, thus showcasing our creativity and ingenuity.

Tried as I might, I could not concentrate. My mind dwelled on the article in the paper. How dare that woman pretend to befriend me just to write a scathing article. And how did she get a photo of me? That picture looked like it had been taken last night. The more I pondered over it, the more I realized… It had! As I thought back to the séance, it occurred to me that she and Lily must have set up cameras, and probably miniature microphones, around the room to record everything that had happened. This had been planned from the beginning.

I spent so much time fuming over last night's events, that I ignored my assignment.

"Time!" said the professor.

I looked at my tablet and realized that I hadn't even started to manipulate the audio file. While others uploaded their new creation to the same site we had downloaded the original file from, I just packed my tablet away in my bag and left. There was no point in uploading my file. I hadn't done anything with it.

I burst out of the building into the cold, crisp February air. My romantic getaway with Greg seemed like a distant memory, even though it had only been a few days ago. My quick steps crunched the layer of snow, which had fallen while I was in class, beneath my feet as I gripped my bag close to me, ignoring all those who passed me, staring and pointing in my direction. Great. Now I was famous, and not in a good way.

My phone buzzed. I looked at it. Jackie had sent me a text telling me to get my butt over to work, now. I quickened my pace and half-jogged, half-walked through the ankle-deep snow. The Candle Shoppe wasn't far, just a few blocks, from campus. I didn't mind walking to work once in a while. On days like these, Greg would drop me off at the college and I walked to work to meet up with Jackie, who would give me a ride home. It worked out well.

As I hurried down the sidewalk, a police car passed me, its lights flashing, though no sirens. That couldn't be good. It turned right, heading in the same direction as the Candle Shoppe. Not caring if I fell on the ice, I ran the rest of the way to work, pleading with the universe that the Candle Shoppe hadn't been broken into again. Once I turned the corner, I stopped. Three police cars were parked outside of the flower shop, which was next door to the Candle Shoppe. There had been another break-in.

Chapter 5

I rushed to the Candle Shoppe, ignoring the officers that tried to stop me.

"Mel!"

I stopped upon hearing Jackie's voice. "What happened?"

"The flower shop next door was broken into sometime last night."

"What?" I said, shocked that two break-ins would take place in almost the exact spot and in such a short amount of time. "Was anything taken?"

"It doesn't look like it," replied Jackie. "I had only just gotten here when all of the cops showed up."

I couldn't believe it. First the Candle Shop is ransacked, then the flower store next to it is broken into and everything is tossed around. If it wasn't a thief, in the conventional sense, then who was doing it? None of it added up. Why break into a place and not steal from it?

"What is going on here, Mel?" asked Jackie.

"I don't know," I said as I watched Detective Shorts question the owner to the flower shop.

Someone walked through the gathered crowd and past the police that scurried about doing their job. As I watched him, I remembered that I had seen him yesterday, and he was the same man I had seen off and on in the Candle Shoppe since the day I had started working there, but I had never thought about it until now.

"Do you think he might know something?" I asked Jackie.

"I don't see how," said Jackie.

"He was in the flower shop yesterday, watching everything as the police conducted their investigation. And I know I have seen him several times in the store. Doesn't he look familiar?"

"Now that you mention it, he does seem somewhat familiar. Might be a repeat customer," Jackie said, paying more attention to the police than the man I stayed focused on.

"Miss Summers?" Detective Shorts had walked up to me.

"I didn't see anything," I replied, automatically. "I was at the college, but you might try asking…" I stopped speaking when I turned to point at the man I had seen only to discover that he had disappeared; probably run off.

"I'm not here to speak to you about the break-in next door."

My head snapped up. This was new. Most times, Detective Shorts wanted to speak to me about a murder I witnessed, or got involved in because of a helpful ghost, but never to just talk.

"Walk with me," said the detective.

Jackie gave me an *don't-ask-me* look, when I glanced at her, shaking her head, while I followed Detective Shorts away from the crowd.

"What's wrong?" I asked.

He showed me his smartphone and the same article was on it that I had read earlier in the paper while in the college cafeteria.

"I didn't…"

"I don't blame you," said Detective Shorts. "I knew I had seen her somewhere before. Her name is Jillian Modsen. She works for the local paper and has aspirations to be a national news anchor. Somehow, she learned of you and has now fixated on you as a story."

"I didn't know!"

"Just be careful," warned Detective Shorts. "Notoriety like this can ruin reputations and lives."

An officer walked up to us, calling the detective's name and he left me standing there alone on the sidewalk. I glanced across the street and thought I saw someone staring right at me, but as I focused on him, he tossed his cigarette aside, shoved his hands in his pockets, and hurried down the walk. I was about to chase after him when Jackie ran up to me, stopping me.

"So, Mr. Stilton says that we should just take the day off. He's not going to open today—and who can blame him? Especially with this mess."

I didn't say anything.

"What's wrong?" asked Jackie, noticing my lack of interest in the robbery next door.

I pulled out my phone and looked up the article that Jillian had written about me and handed it to her.

"That witch!" shouted Jackie.

I was about to agree with her when my phone rang. It was Tiny. "Mel, here."

"Mel?" Oh boy! Tiny did not sound well. "I need you"—a series of coughs interrupted his statement—"to come over here."

"Sure," I said. "Are you all right? You sound terrible."

"It's nothing."

"It doesn't sound like nothing."

"It's just a cold," said Tiny. "But come over, please, I need to speak with you."

"Be right there." I hung up. "We need to go to Tiny's, but first, let's pick up some chicken noodle soup," I said to Jackie.

"Tiny's? What's wrong?"

"He wants to see me."

"And the soup?"

"He's not feeling well."

We said good-bye to Mr. Stilton, who told us to just leave, and got into Jackie's car. We stopped at a local diner and picked up a quart of their chicken noodle soup to go, before heading over to Tiny's.

"Tiny?" I called, opening the door to his apartment, which was above a car repair garage. A fit of coughing answered me. "Tiny?"

"Over here," said a hoarse voice.

I stepped inside his apartment, but Jackie stopped in the doorway. "Come on," I said to her.

"I don't want to get sick," she said, hugging her arms in close and jumping from foot to foot in an effort to keep warm, despite the frigid wind.

"You're going to freeze out there," I replied.

Relenting, and turning blue from the cold, Jackie came inside and I shut the door.

"Hey," I said to Tiny, who huddled on the couch with a blanket wrapped around him and five boxes of half-full tissues situated around him, along with mounds of used ones. I handed him the carton of soup and a plastic spoon. "Here."

"I'm not sick," protested Tiny.

Jackie scoffed, voicing her disagreement.

"Sure you aren't," I said, "which is why you are wrapped up tighter than a caterpillar in its cocoon and have a bunch of snot infested tissues on the floor."

In a huff, Tiny snatched the soup, popping off the plastic lid, and ate a spoonful.

"What's up?" I asked him.

He plopped his tablet in front of me with this morning's front page news on its screen, and an ugly picture of me. "And Elise"—he tossed a newspaper at me and I caught it—"brought this in this morning."

I grimaced. I knew there was no way I would be able to keep them from seeing it, but had hoped that it would still be a while.

"I ran into her yesterday when the Candle Shoppe had been broken into. She acted all…"

"What!" Tiny's tone told me that he hadn't known about yesterday's events, which meant he must have really been sick; it's the only way he could have been out of the loop.

"Sorry," I said. "I should have told you."

"Oh, don't worry about it," said Tiny, waving away my concern. "It wouldn't have done much good. I slept all day yesterday." He took some more mouthfuls of the steaming soup and I could tell by his facial expression that it helped ease his sore throat.

"She acted all scared," I continued, "and I was just trying to be friendly. I didn't know that she was some reporter. Or that she planned this."

"You need to be careful, Mel," said Tiny. "Judging by that piece, this woman means business."

"But why?" asked Jackie; she still stood near the door, not wanting to get too close to Tiny, afraid of catching his cold.

"Oh, who knows?" said Tiny, releasing a small cough, despite his efforts at trying to suppress it. "I don't know her that well myself, which means she hasn't done much to make waves, until now."

I frowned. This didn't bode well.

"Now, tell me about this break in at the Candle Shoppe," said Tiny.

I relayed the details of how I had arrived at work to open the store and found it ransacked, but nothing appeared to have been stolen; and according to Jackie, Mr. Stilton has accounted for everything so far. With each passing second, Tiny's face became more and more worried.

"Yeah, but the flower store next door was broken into last night," Jackie said when I had finished. "And nothing was taken."

"Strange thief," mumbled Tiny.

"Or thieves," said Jackie.

At that moment, the door opened and in marched Elise with her arms full of shopping bags. Jackie took a few and helped her into the kitchen.

"Thanks," said Elise. "I got you," she said to Tiny, "cough drops, nasal decongestants, cough syrup, and some herbal tea."

Tiny groaned. "I want a beer."

"Not while you're sick, you won't," Elise scolded him, placing her hands on her hips. "And this herbal stuff won't kill you."

Tony grunted in response.

"Mel, Jackie, good to see you," said Elise, ignoring Tiny's grumblings. "What are you two girls up to?"

"Tiny called about this morning's article," I replied.

"I told him not to bother you about it." Elise gave him a reprimanding glare and Tiny looked down at his bare feet. "Lord knows you have enough things to worry about. Like a wedding."

"Yes, a wedding!" Rachel popped into the room, flinging loose papers everywhere. "I am going to be your bridesmaid! Or the maid of honor."

I covered my face with my gloved hand while the others stared at me with a mixture of confusion and comprehension. They had become used to some of Rachel's antics, but her habit of popping in and out still surprised them, and me, sometimes.

"Well?" said Rachel.

"Rachel," I replied, "I really can't be thinking about this right now." I showed her the tablet with the article on the screen.

"That…" She left.

"Rachel?" asked Elise.

"Is gone," I said. "I feel somewhat sorry for that Jillian." My mind fiddled with ideas of what Rachel had planned for her, though I must admit that I wasn't broken up about it.

"We should probably go too," said Jackie.

"No stay," croaked Tiny.

"So that they can catch your cold?" said Elise. "I don't think so."

Jackie and I said our good-byes and left, with Elise telling me to not worry about Jillian. With nothing else to do, we went home where I spent the rest of the day and evening catching up on school work, wondering where Rachel had disappeared to.

Chapter 6

The next morning I awoke to a gray and dreary day with sleet pelting the glass of my window, making little *tick, tick, ticks*. I moaned when I remembered that I had to go out in it within a couple of hours. I was so sick and tired of winter and just wanted spring to arrive, or at least the snow melt.

"Mel, you up?" Jackie knocked on my bedroom door.

"Yeah," I replied, my voice still hoarse from having just woken up, "I'll be ready to go in a minute."

"Go? Go where?"

"Work," I said, rubbing the sand from my eyes.

"We don't have to go to work today, remember?"

My eyes popped open. That was right. Mr. Stilton had decided to just close up for the next day or two because of the two break-ins. But why would someone break into a place of business and not take anything, much less leave the cash register alone? I needed to know why the Candle Shoppe was targeted. It was where I worked.

I jumped out of bed and flung my door open, running right into Jackie.

"Whoa! Slow down there, Mel!"

"Jackie," I said, "we need to go to the Candle Shoppe."

"And do what, exactly?"

"Investigate the break-in."

Jackie gave me a reproachful look and I couldn't blame her; I was about to drag her into another one of my private investigations.

"I still have the key," I said; and I did, since I forgot to return it to Mr. Stilton during all of the excitement from two days ago.

"Mel, are you sure you want to get involved in this?"

"I'm already involved," I said, throwing on some jeans and a t-shirt. "I'm the one who found the store like that, and yesterday the flower shop next to it was broken into, but nothing was taken. Don't you find it odd?"

"Well, I'll admit that it does seem to go against the parameters of being a thief," admitted Jackie.

"And it was the place where we work that was violated," I continued, hoping that it would be enough to convince Jackie.

"You do have a point," said Jackie, "and I would like to be able to go back there without wondering if the same person is going to break in again. I just… something just isn't right here."

I understood her sentiment. I had been thinking the same. "I'll buy you a gooey, jelly filled donut for breakfast."

"With strawberry filling?" asked Jackie.

"Yep." Okay, maybe I was being a little conniving by bribing Jackie, but I knew how to get her to come along; besides, she was just as interested in this as I was.

I rushed out of my room and found a jelly donut floating in midair.

"Surprise!" Rachel materialized behind it, holding the gooey, sugary goodness in her hand. "For you, my dear." She handed the jelly donut to Jackie, who wasted no time in shoving it into her mouth.

"What," she said over a mouthful of donut when I looked at her with a shocked expression. "I'm hungry. And she did offer."

"Rachel," I said, "where did you get the donut?"

"From the bakery, of course," replied Rachel as though the answer should have been obvious. "Don't worry. I paid for it!"

"How?" For some reason, I didn't think she had any currency to pay for such things.

"With the money I took from your wallet."

What? I seized my purse and yanked out my wallet, opening it to find that the cash I had in there was gone.

"What?" said Rachel. "You were going to be buying her one anyway, so I did it for you, that way you can get started on your investigation."

"Next time, ask.," I said to her.

I pulled out my phone and texted Greg to see if he was up. He was. I let him know that Jackie and I were going to the Candle Shoppe to do some snooping and asked if he wanted to join us. Within thirty seconds, a knock sounded on the door and I opened it to find him standing there, bundled up and with his keys in his hand.

"There is no way I am letting you two go over there alone," he said.

I gave him a big kiss.

"Oh get a room you two," joked Rachel. "Oh my goodness! I almost forgot. I have somewhere to be!" She vanished, leaving us alone in my apartment, wondering what it was that was so important, that she chose to pass up a chance to do some amateur sleuthing.

Without delaying any further, the three of us trooped down to the parking area and piled into Greg's car, arriving at the Candle Shoppe within 15 minutes. I remarked at how light the traffic was, since this time in the morning was usually busy,

"You should pull into the back alley," I said, tugging the store key out of my pocket.

The car slowed.

"What's wrong?" I looked up and my hopes of being able to look around the Candle Shoppe without being bothered were dashed. For the third time this week, police cars were parked outside of the strip where the Candle Shoppe was, their red and blue lights flashing so bright that it lit up the dark day.

"Oh, no. Not again," moaned Jackie.

"You should park over there," I said, pointing at a place across the street that was well away from the police cruisers.

"It looks like it was the hobby store this time," said Jackie.
I opened the car door.

"What are you doing?" demanded Greg.

"I'm going to have a look," I replied.

"I'm coming with you," said Greg.

"No," I stopped him, "you should stay here. If we all go over there, it will attract attention. I'll only be a minute. I just want to know if our suspicions are correct."

"All right," said Greg. "Be quick. The longer we're parked here, the more attention we'll attract."

I jumped out of the car, wrapping my coat tight around me as the sleet seemed to soak right through it, and hurried across the street, doing my best not to slip and slide on the thin layer of ice, blending into the small crowd that had gathered. As I watched the police dart about in the freezing rain—none too pleased either—I saw that Jackie's guess had been correct; the little hobby store had been broken into this time. Detective Shorts stood in the rain, his coat soaked just like everyone here, directing the officers and questioning the owner of the store.

"Was anything taken, do you know?" I asked the man next to me in an innocent tone, hoping that I came across as a curious bystander.

"Blundering little waif," said the man, "the film is safe."

Huh? Did he just speak in a rhyme? I turned and looked at the man next to me, jumping back in surprise. It was the same man that I had seen loitering around. Sure, I had seen him before since I started working at the Candle Shoppe, but he never stuck around, and I don't think I had seen him this many times in just a few days, much less hear him speak. A few taunts and jeers from some teenagers on their way to the school bus stop peeled my attention away from the man standing next to me. When I looked back, he had gone.

That was odd. What was it with this guy and disappearing so quickly? And why was it he only showed up to watch the police conduct another investigation into another break-in? Before I had time to think about it, a honking horn pulled me from my musing. Greg and Jackie were ready to go. Knowing I wouldn't be able to get away with searching the Candle Shoppe on my own, I started for the car, but as I took a second step, Detective Shorts called my name.

"Miss Summers!" He hurried away from the entrance of the hobby store and shoved his way through the crowd to me. "Miss Summers, I need to speak with you."

"I wasn't snooping," I said. "I was just coming to work when I noticed all of this."

Detective Shorts gave me a disbelieving look. Oh, yeah, he knew me too well. "Let's just say I actually believe you, even though I had talked to Mr. Stilton about ten minutes ago and he informed me that he had decided to not open today."

He caught me. "What can I do for you?" I asked him, changing the subject and curious as to why he singled me out of the crowd, since it was obvious that he wasn't there to chastise me.

Detective Shorts took my arm and led me away from the others to a somewhat empty area of the sidewalk, next to waist high plant boxes with the shriveled remains of the flowers that used to thrive in them. He showed me his phone with another article posted about me online by none other than Jillian Modsen. Oh no, I thought, this could not be good.

Robberies of Local Businesses. Where is Our Psychic?

Jillian Modsen

The past two days has seen two break-ins of locally owned stores (The Candle Shoppe and the Flower Boutique) which have the police baffled as, rumor has it, nothing was taken. The detective on the case, Detective Shorts, was seen talking to Mellow Summers, our resident psychic, on the mornings that both stores were found ransacked. One wonders how much help the self-proclaimed psychic will be since she failed to predict that her own place of employment would be targeted by the thief/thieves.

Though, there has been speculation that perhaps Mellow Summers herself is behind these break-ins. She has been seen at both places where the incidents took place. Indeed, since the two break-ins, witnesses have spotted Miss Summers talking to the detective in charge, though it is still unknown if she has been brought in as a consultant, or is a prime suspect.

If another incident should occur, can the police truly call themselves responsible by consulting with a psychic who cannot tell them about the robberies before they happen?

Detective Shorts took his phone before I had a chance to smash it on the icy ground in disgust. That little... What did I ever do to her?

"That was posted at around four this morning, online, and printed in this morning's local paper."

"Why is she doing this?"

"Miss Summers," said the detective, "I urge you to be careful."

"I never even spoke to her yesterday!"

Detective Shorts pulled me further away from the crowd, urging me to keep my voice low and to not let my anger get the better of me. "I never accused you of doing so, but this woman has fixated on you."

"But why?"

"There have been cases of individuals claiming to be mediums or psychics, but were later proven to be frauds merely wanting their 15 minutes of fame."

"So she thinks I'm a fake?"

"I think she intends to put the idea in people's minds that you are and make a name for herself. This Jillian Modsen is a shrewd woman who wants to make her mark on the world, starting with you. I want you to be careful. This kind of notoriety puts a target on your back."

"Target?"

"Yes. Not everyone is open to the idea of mediums

and psychics, but also, someone who might have a grudge to settle, because of a case you helped solve, may get the idea to do something about it. I think you ought to not go out as much."

I lowered my head, mulling over Detective Shorts' concerns, wishing that I had never met Jillian Modsen. "Do you think I'm a fake?" I asked.

"No... I..." Detective Shorts' voice trailed off as his eyes drifted away from me and to a slow moving black sedan. I didn't think much of it, figuring that the driver was just being careful, considering all of the people that had gathered to watch the police and assuage their curiosity; but Detective Shorts kept his eyes fixed on the car and the driver's side window that rolled down.

Before I could react, Detective Shorts grabbed me, flinging me to the frozen cement of the sidewalk, covering me with his body as three shots rang out. The glass of the store window above us shattered, raining shards of would-be-knives around us. Squealing tires filled the air, their high pitch hurting my ears, as the black sedan sped off. I didn't get the license plate. I hoped someone had. The distinct sound of sirens cut through the commotion when an officer reached his car and took off after the sedan.

Screams surrounded us as people shrieked in fear and ran off, afraid that they might be targeted next and ignoring the detective and me as we lay on the ground. Once I had made certain that the sedan would not return, I shuffled out from underneath Detective Shorts. He didn't move.

"Detective?" I said, shaking him. My coat felt wet. I pulled it tight and found blobs of blood on its bottom. I didn't feel any pain so it wasn't mine. "Detective?"

As I turned him over onto his back, I saw the blood on his partially open coat. Adrenaline and panic rushed through me as I pulled out my phone, fumbling with it and dropping it on the wet sidewalk. Just as I started dialing 911, two officers reached us, one speaking into his radio and the other pulling me away from the detective.

"Mel!"

Both Jackie and Greg screamed my name, running up to me, but the officers pushed them back, while three others arrived. "I'm sorry, but you can't be here," said one.

"She's my girlfriend!" shouted Greg, ramming his way through, but two more officers seized him and held him back.

"Sir, I need you to calm down. Please! You need to let us and the paramedics do their jobs."

Jackie grabbed Greg's wrist and pulled him back, calming him down. She knew that there was nothing they could do, except let the paramedics, when they arrived, do their work. I caught her eye while she and Greg stepped away, hoping that she got my message: I was fine. She nodded in response.

"Ma'am. Ma'am," said the officer that had pulled me away from Detective Shorts, "are you hurt?"

I shook my head.

"Are you sure?"

I nodded. While the officer looked away for a second,

I sent a quick text to Greg's and Jackie's phone (*I'm fine.*), reinforcing that I was okay physically. Jackie sent me a happy face, while Greg watched me with a worried expression.

The police officer that had asked me if I was okay, led me to the side, telling me to stay there until the ambulance arrived. I obeyed. My mind flooded with questions and different scenarios, each worse than the one before, as I watched, stone-faced, the scene unfold before me, the only noise in my head being the sirens of the ambulance as it pulled up.

Chapter 7

I sat in the waiting room at the hospital with both Jackie and Greg seated on each side of me, all of us quiet. What could we say? The paramedics had me ride in the ambulance with Detective Shorts—Greg and Jackie followed—to make sure that I wasn't injured as well. I thought back to how they worked on Detective Shorts, but he remained unconscious, while one paramedic asked me questions, doing his best to be patient with my inaudible whispers for answers. Once we had arrived at the hospital, I was checked over by a doctor, while the detective was wheeled into surgery, and cleared. It turned out that the bullets missed me and the detective took the full impact. All I suffered was few bumps and bruises.

Detective Shorts had no immediate family in the area, so I decided to wait in the waiting room. Someone ought to wait for him. I replayed the incident over and over in my mind. Why would someone try to kill Detective Shorts? If the attempt had been connected to the break-ins, it didn't make sense, since nothing had been taken, there were no prints, and the police had no leads. Taking a potshot at a detective was the surest way to make sure you got caught, if it was, in fact, the one who was responsible for the break-ins who did the shooting.

And where was Rachel? Why wasn't she there? Why didn't she stop the whole thing from happening? *Don't blame her, Mel,* I scolded myself, *Rachel can't know everything.* But I was curious as to why she had rushed off before we left for the Candle Shoppe.

"Here," said Greg, breaking the silence.

"What's this?" I asked.

"The information you wanted me to look up. I had Jack do some digging and he said that this should be Tom's number. I know this isn't really a good time, but Rachel isn't here right now and you said you wanted it to be a surprise."

"It's fine," I said, taking the slip of paper with the number on it and shoving it in my pocket.

The doctor walked into the waiting room. We all rose to our feet in nervous anticipation.

"He's out of surgery," said the doctor. "The bullet hit no major arteries and barring any post-surgery complications, I expect him to make a full recovery. He is still unconscious, but if you wish to see him, you can. The nurse, here, will take you to him."

"Thank you, doctor," said Greg.

The nurse led us into his hospital room and I cringed,

seeing him lying there hooked up to tubes. I placed the bag of his personal effects on the tray next to his bed, A nurse had given them to me and I accepted them for safekeeping. Who else was going to hang onto his stuff?

"Someone should stay here with him," I said. "It wouldn't be right not to."

"I'll stay," Greg volunteered. "You should go home and rest."

"I don't think I can," I said.

"Come on, Mel," said Jackie, "you've got to be tired."

More shaken up than tired. I didn't think I could sleep, even if I wanted to. I shivered. Greg wrapped me in his arms and held me close. Now that the adrenaline from earlier had worn off, everything hit me at once and my body felt cold.

"Here"—Greg handed Jackie his car keys—"take her home."

"What about you?" I asked.

"I'll take a cab if I need to, but for now, I'll stay here until he wakes up."

"Come on, hun," said Jackie, urging me out the door. "There isn't anything else you can do here."

I allowed myself to be led outside. She and Greg were both right: there was nothing else I could do at the moment and I was in no position to do anything anyway. As we walked into the main lobby of the hospital, we met a familiar face that I did not want to see: Jillian.

"Mel," she greeted with a pasty smile.

"Only my friends call me that," I spat.

"There's no need to get nasty," said Jillian.

"No need?" I said, but Jackie cut in.

"Leave her alone! How dare you write those articles about her. Do you delight in destroying someone's life?"

"You brought it upon yourself," said Jillian.

"Excuse me?" I said. "I was just trying to help you and you stabbed me in the back."

"You're the one who claims to be psychic," said Jillian.

"I never made any such…" I began.

"Get away from us," Jackie's voice took on a dangerous tone and pushed me towards the door.

"I noticed that your abilities failed to save your detective friend," said Jillian.

I turned to say something, but at that precise moment, Rachel popped into the room, shoving Jillian out of her way, and barreled into me, embracing me in a giant hug.

"MEL!" she yelled, causing a few of the hospital staff to look in our direction, while almost knocking me off my feet from the force of her impact. "I just found out! I can't believe… are you all right? You must be totally shaken up."

Jillian watched me with interest as Rachel turned me about, looking me over; though, it looked as though I was being manipulated by thin air.

"Rachel," I whispered, nodding in Jillian's direction.

"So this is the little tramp that's been writing all of those dishonest articles about you." Rachel crossed her arms and looked Jillian over, not that Jillian could see her. "What's your problem with my friend, huh?"

Jillian's face indicated that she either hadn't heard Rachel, or didn't want to acknowledge that she had.

"What is your problem with me, Jillian?" I asked. "What did I ever do to you?"

"Nothing personally," answered Jillian, "but I know your type."

"Her type?" said Jackie; her eyes narrowed.

"I've run into people like you," said Jillian, closing the distance between us. "You pretend to have special mediumistic abilities, preying upon the innocent, but you're nothing special. You're no psychic, Mellow Summers, and I intend to prove it."

"You don't want to go down this road," I said.

"Is that a threat?" asked Jillian. "You know, someone tampered with my car soon after the first article I wrote was published."

"That's it," said Jackie, tearing me away from Jillian. "We're leaving."

"You're a fraud!" shouted Jillian after us. "And I'm going to prove..." Rachel shoved Jillian to the floor, silencing her. Jillian glanced around, but could find no explanation for what had happened, and Jackie and I were several yards away, heading towards the parking lot.

"I don't like her," said Rachel, so we both could hear her, as we climbed into Greg's car.

"You and me both," Jackie replied through gritted teeth.

"Where were you this morning?" I asked Rachel once we started down the road.

"I'll tell you later."

"But..." I began.

"Later," said Rachel, cutting me off. "You need some rest first."

And that was that. Rachel and Jackie were in agreement and there was nothing I could do to change their minds. Once we got back to the apartment, they put me in bed and I fell asleep as my body finally relaxed from the day's horrifying events.

Chapter 8

Nightmares plagued me as I tossed and turned in a vain attempt to sleep, dreaming about what had happened and about hearing the gunfire and being pushed to the ground with Detective Shorts' dead weight. I woke up, bolting upright in my bed, sweat covering me, making my pajamas cling to my skin. As I tried to calm my breathing, I realized I wasn't alone.

"You must be having some terrible dreams to make you wake up like that," said Rachel, standing in the far corner of my room.

"What are you doing here?" I asked, not trying to be rude, but was curious.

"Jackie thought that someone should keep an eye on you, but she was yawning so much that I told her to go to bed. I'd ask you what you were dreaming about, but I can probably guess."

"Did anyone see the car?" I asked.

"No, though Greg got a partial license plate, which he gave to the cops."

"What did Jillian mean when she said that someone had tampered with her car?" I asked.

Rachel shifted, avoiding my gaze and my question.

"Rachel?"

"Well…" began Rachel, "she had a little, teeny, tiny bit of car trouble."

"And that bit of car trouble had some help, didn't it?"

"Well she deserved it!"

"Rachel…"

"I'm not sorry!"

"What did you do to her car, anyway?" I asked.

"Sugar in the gas tank."

A part of me laughed. That would ruin a car.

"By the way, I owe you a bag of sugar."

"Jackie was wondering what had happened to it."

"And while she waited for the tow truck," continued Rachel, speaking about Jillian, "I threw snowballs at her. If she doesn't believe in ghosts now, she will by the time I'm through with her."

I gave her a reproachful look, though a part of me was pleased that she had done that, since Jillian had made me a laughing stock around town with her scathing articles.

"You should go back to sleep," said Rachel.

"I don't think I can."

"Tell you what, you lay down and close your eyes

while I go get you some warm milk. That was my mother's cure-all for sleeplessness. If you are still awake when I get back, then I'll let you get up and I'll accompany you on your investigation."

"Something tells me that you are going to come with me anyway," I said.

"Just snuggle under those blankets," ordered Rachel.

I obeyed. You can't argue with a ghost, especially when that ghost is named Rachel. I laid back down, tucking the comforter under my chin. If Rachel did return with a glass of warm milk, I never knew it, since I had fallen back asleep.

I awoke when the sun had just come up, its faint light trying to poke through the shade that covered my window. I didn't see Rachel, but had a feeling that she was still around. After dressing, and failing to comb out the tangled mess that was my hair, I shuffled out of my bedroom and into the living room, where I parked my butt on the cushiony couch.

A tray with a plateful of eggs, bacon, toast, and a cup of coffee appeared in my lap, handed to me by Rachel, who wore an apron around her waist. "Breakfast is served."

Jackie moseyed into the room, yawning so big that a hornets could have built a nest in her mouth. I gaped at her. This had to have been the first time in the years I have known her where she did not look picture perfect. Her normally smooth and perfectly groomed hair resembled a gnarly wad of tangled wires, a few strands flopping in her face. She scratched her side and yawned some more. "Morning," she said.

"You look like you've had about as much sleep as me," I said.

"Uh-huh." Jackie snatched a piece of bacon from my plate and chewed on it, her eyes still half closed from wanting to go back to sleep.

"You know, if you wanted some bacon," Rachel said to Jackie, her hands on her hips, "all you had to do was ask." She huffed as she stormed back into the kitchen and brought out another plate of bacon, eggs, and toast, shoving it into Jackie's unsuspecting hands.

"We need to find out who was trying to kill Detective Shorts," I said.

Jackie gulped down her mouthful of eggs. "I knew you were going to say that."

"We can't just…"

"I'm not saying we should," said Jackie, interrupting me. "Let's be extra careful on this one. You could have been hit yesterday."

"I know," I said. "I just can't let this go. It's too odd. Three shops get broken into, all on the same stretch of real estate, but nothing is taken. Then, someone takes a few shots at Detective Shorts."

"Eat first," said Jackie, and Rachel nodded her head in approval, "then we will go see Jack. Greg got a partial license plate number. Maybe Jack can help us look up a few matches."

My phone rang. I started to hurry over to it, but Rachel had beaten me to it, snatching my phone and dumping it in my lap. "Hello," I said.

"Mel?" Tiny's voice sounded even worse than it did

when I had taken over the chicken noodle soup. "I heard about yesterday. I'm coming over."

"No, you're not," I said. "You sound terrible and the best thing for you to do is to stay home and rest."

"Not while someone is taking shots at you," argued Tiny through a fit of garbled coughs. "Now, I'm coming over."

"Tiny, the best thing you can do is stay home."

"I'll handle this," said Rachel as she vanished.

A few seconds later I heard Tiny on the other end and it sounded as though someone was beating him up.

"Hey! What are you... leave... I don't... OKAY!"

"Now you stay in that bed until I tell you otherwise," I heard Rachel yell at him as I pressed the phone to my ear.

Rachel reappeared in the living room. "There," she said. "That should take care of him. The idiot, wanting to come over here with his cold, as though you need to catch it too."

"On second thought, Mel," said Tiny over the phone, "I think I will stay here, but if anything else happens, I'm sending one of my boys over."

"Thanks, Tiny," I said. "You just concentrate on getting better."

Tiny harumphed and hung up, no doubt not liking the fact that he just got scolded and ordered about by a ghost.

Once I had finished talking to Tiny, I called Greg and he answered on the first ring. "Greg? How's Detective Shorts."

"Still unconscious," he replied. I could tell that he hadn't gotten much sleep.

"If you'd like, I'm sure Rachel wouldn't mind keeping an eye on him while you come home and go to bed."

"Can't," said Greg. "I've got to get to work in a couple of hours."

"I'll stay with him," said Rachel, tearing off her apron. "No problem!"

"Are you sure you can't just call in?" I asked Greg.

"No," said Greg. "I used up some vacation time for last weekend and I only get a certain amount of sick days. I'll be fine. I'll just take a cab to work and then take one to get home."

"Are you sure?"

"Don't worry about me."

"Okay, well, Jackie says that you got a partial license plate number from that car yesterday. We were going to go to Jack and see if he could try finding some matches."

"Good idea," said Greg. "You two head down there. I'll call Jack and see to it that he doesn't give you any grievances about being asked to help."

"Love you," I said.

"Love you back," said Greg.

"AWW," said Rachel, "you two are so sweet to one another." My face turned red.

"All right," said Rachel. "I'll go relieve your fiancé and no one is going to get past the door to the detective's room."

"Except maybe the doctors and nurses," mumbled Jackie over a mouthful of toast.

"Except the doctors and nurses," agreed Rachel.

"And maybe us," continued Jackie.

"And you guys, of course," Rachel said.

"And maybe the police officer on guard there," Jackie added.

"And maybe—are you about finished?"

Jackie nodded; a few crumbs dropped in her lap as she did.

"I know what to do!" Rachel disappeared with a gust of wind this time, tussling Jackie's mop of bed-hair.

We finished our breakfast and left for the police station. There weren't many people there. It seemed as though everyone had either taken the day off, or every available person was searching for the man who had shot Detective Shorts. Jackie and I snuck in past the front desk, which wasn't difficult since the lady who was supposed to be there had left, and hurried down into the basement where Jack's office was. He worked as their IT guy and was responsible for making certain that their computers and database remained up to date and secure, which was why we often came to him for assistance in looking up information, besides the fact that he was also Greg's cousin.

When we arrived in his office, Jackie and I found Jack waiting for us. He held up a manila envelope without even looking up from the computer screen.

"Thanks," I said.

I opened the envelope and pulled out a list of possible matches to the license plate that Greg had gotten a partial number off of, with Jackie leaning over my shoulder eager to know where to begin. Five possibilities.

"Is there anything else you can tell us?" I asked Jack.

"Nope," said Jack, still glued to his computer.

"Are we bothering you?" Jackie asked in a sarcastic tone.

"Yep," replied Jack.

Jackie raised her hand to smack him, no doubt taking

lessons from Rachel on how to get a point across, but I seized it and pulled her back, shaking my head. She jerked her arm free, relenting.

"Let's go," I said to her. "Thanks again, Jack," I called to him as Jackie and I left.

We started with the first address on the list. It took us to a small bungalow style house in a secluded neighborhood. When I saw the car with the matching license plate in the driveway, I knew that it wasn't the one we searched for. The vehicle was a 20-year-old corvette, its rusty fender being held in place by duct tape and bungee cords.

Jackie checked it off the list and we headed to possibility number two. An abandoned looking house greeted us. Its slanted roof sagged under the weight of the snow we've had falling at a constant pace for the last four weeks. A similar mound of wet snow filled the single lane driveway. We got out of the car and walked up the driveway, forging our way through knee-deep snow. I had already suspected that this was not the car and as I ran my hand across the back, exposing the license plate from underneath the snow, my suspicions were confirmed.

"Let's go," I said. "This isn't the car. There is no way someone parked it here yesterday and all of this snow showed up."

Jackie agreed and we moved to the next place, which was at a rundown apartment complex. We found the third car with ease, but my hopes at it being the one we wanted were dashed. Not only was it not a black sedan, but the car itself was up on cinderblocks with its tires missing. So much for that idea.

Possibility number four proved to be another dead end. When we arrived, a tow truck was dragging the car (though it was a black sedan) away and the owner had informed us that she hadn't been able to get it to start for the last two days.

"Should we check the last one on the list?" asked Jackie, doubtful about how helpful it would prove.

"Might as well," I replied.

We drove to the final address on the list, which took us to a more well-to-do area of the city, with nice fenced in homes that were all part of a gated community. I slowed the car, unsure if we would be allowed in. Most of these communities require people to have an access code, or some sort of permission to enter. Hoping that I needed neither, I approached the gate on the right and a guard stopped us.

"Name?" he asked, all businesslike.

"Mellow Summers," I said.

"What address are you visiting?" he asked.

Before I had a chance to answer, a delivery van pulled up to the second gate (the one on the left) and the guard waved him through.

"We're with him," I said.

"What?"

"Yeah," I replied. "Look I have an order here in the trunk for the party that he is also delivering to. It's my first week on the job and if I don't make this delivery I'll…"

"All right. All right. Don't get your coat in a knot." He pressed a button from inside the guardhouse and the gate opened. "Next time you are making a delivery here, be sure to call ahead of time to get a pass."

"Thank you so much," I said, acting grateful and appreciative of the guard's niceness.

Before he had a chance to change his mind and ask more questions, I sped off and followed the winding road to the street we searched for, while Jackie watched the house numbers.

"There it is," she said, pointing at a two-story, dull yellow house with white trim.

I parked across the street. I didn't want to attract attention. A black sedan sat in the driveway. I shut off the car and hurried over to it with Jackie right behind me; the piece of paper with the license plate number on it waved in the wind as I clutched it. I read the license plate number and it matched.

"Look," I said to Jackie.

"Holy… Mel, I think you've found it."

The door to the garage opened with harsh voices spilling from it. Jackie and I ran back to the car, ducking low in an effort to not be seen. When I looked back, I knew we hadn't been spotted.

"We should call the police," said Jackie. "They have a number that you can call anonymously. We should call it and let them know that the car is here."

I agreed and had just pulled out my cell phone when another car pulled up and a man and a woman stepped out. They had to have been detectives. Their gait and the way they carried themselves displayed as much; and one of them pointed at the license plate on the car. Jackie and I watched as they questioned the two men, one younger and one much older, who had ceased their argument for the moment.

"Yeah, that's my car," said the older one, "but I haven't been here all week."

"Does anyone have access to your car?" asked the female detective.

"My son does. Wait a minute? Are you implying that we had something to do with that shooting yesterday?"

"Sir," said the other detective, "we're going to need you and your son to come with us."

"Now, wait a minute!"

"Sir…"

A struggle ensued as the older man put up a fight, shouting about his rights and how he had nothing to do yesterday's attempt on Detective Shorts' life. After the detectives had put both men in the back of their car, they left, having never seen me or Jackie.

"I think we should go."

So did I. I started the car and high-tailed it out of there, but as we left, we passed a beautiful two story home, with a wraparound porch, and tended shrubbery that glistened from the snow that draped over them. In front of the house, clearing the walkway, was a man. I allowed myself to stare at him a bit, thinking that I had seen him before.

"Mel, pay attention!" Jackie shouted at me.

I snapped my eyes forward, realizing that I was about to rear end a parked car and jerked the wheel, avoiding it by a few inches, but plowed into a snowbank on the side of the road.

"What's gotten into you?" asked Jackie. "You almost hit that car! And it was parked!"

"Sorry," I replied. "I thought I saw someone I recognized." I looked back, but the man had gone, not that I needed have worried because he showed up right outside the driver's window.

"Can't you drive?" he demanded, holding a snow shovel over his right shoulder.

"Uh…"

"You've no business being here," he continued. "This is a closed community. How did you get past the guard?"

I tried to think of a valid excuse, but every possible one that entered my mind sounded more feeble than the last.

"Well?" demanded the man.

"Donald, that will be quite enough," said a woman in a stern voice. "Now get something to help pull them out of this snow pile."

Grumbling, and no doubt angry at having been reprimanded, he stalked off, waving the snow shovel before him.

"I'm sorry," I said. "We didn't mean to scare him. All this ice has made the roads really slippery."

"Oh, don't worry about it." The woman's silver hair blew in the breeze, framing her face a little with the few tendrils that fought against the wind. "Donald can be a little off-putting, but he's harmless."

"We weren't trying to upset your son," I said.

"He's not my son," laughed the woman. "Donald is the gardener. Well, groundskeeper mostly. He helps me with the outdoor tasks that I find I can't do myself anymore."

I felt embarrassed.

"I am Beverly Waverly. I noticed your car sitting on the curb down there."

"We were just…"

"I know who you are, Miss Summers."

Jackie's eyes widened and she made a movement with her hands, telling me to get away from there before we found ourselves facing the police again, though forgetting that we were trapped by a mound of snow.

Beverly must have noticed Jackie's sudden movements because she put her hand out to calm us down. "Don't worry. I'm not going to report you, but you have been making waves in the papers lately." She held up yesterday's newspaper with the second of Jillian's scathing articles about me. "Though I would like to know what brought you here."

"We were just…" I began, but Jackie jumped in and finished my sentence for me.

"Were just working on another case."

I gaped at her. What was she doing?

Beverly's eyes lit up and I realized that Jackie must have sensed something I hadn't: Beverly Waverly was on my side. "Really? And so your abilities led you here?"

"Sort of," I said. She didn't need to know that I had gotten a list of possible matches to the black sedan's license plate from someone employed at the local police department. "My abilities don't always work…"

"To the house down the street there," interrupted Jackie, "but the police have already stopped by."

"Oh, I know. Poor man. He would never do anything, like shooting on a crowd of people. The police must have it wrong, which is why they need you." Beverly looked at me when she said that last part.

"I don't know about that," I said, "but my work was broken into a few days ago and…"

"Where do you work?"

"The Candle Shoppe," I replied. "It's a little store in the center of downtown."

"Yes, I know where it is," said Beverly. "That place used to be a photography studio; well, the entire strip used to be."

"Really?" said Jackie. "I never knew that."

"Well, how could you?" chuckled Beverly. "That was about 20 years ago, back when Roger…" She stopped speaking and her voice choked up a bit.

"Roger?" I asked.

"Someone both my son and I used to know, but that was a long time ago."

Donald rode up on one of those small tractors with a blade for plowing snow attached to the front. It's loud roar filled what silence remained in the air. He jumped off it, carrying a rope in his hands—his gruff and mechanical movements making it clear that he was not thrilled with being forced to pull our car out of the snowbank—and tied one end of the rope around my rear bumper, while the other end was tied to the tractor.

"Gun the engine as I pull you out," he said to me. "And make sure your emergency brake isn't on."

I did as he asked, keeping my eyes on him in the rear-view mirror. When he gave me the signal, I punched the gas pedal just as he tugged on the car with his tractor. My car rocked back and forth a bit, making me somewhat seasick, but with one final pull on his part, and another stomp on the accelerator, my car popped free of the snow mound. It wasn't that stuck, but just needed that little bit of a tug. Once freed, I got out and checked the front end; it wasn't damaged, just a few scrapes in the paint and a couple of dings.

"We really should get going," I said to Jackie more than Beverly.

"I understand," said Beverly. "If you should ever wish to stop by, feel free. My son rarely ever visits me these days and the only company I have is Donald."

I saw the loneliness in her eyes and felt guilty for having to leave her, but we did need to get to the hospital.

"Perhaps we could later in the week," I said. "Is there a number we should call?"

"Oh, don't bother," said Beverly. "I'm always here. I'll leave your names with the guard and instructions to let you in at any time."

"Thanks," I said, shaking her hand.

I got back in the car, avoiding Donald's piercing gaze—he did not look happy—and drove away, being extra careful to not run into any more cars or snowbanks.

"Maybe we ought to stop somewhere to get some lunch."

Rachel popped in the back seat of my car. "Hey!" she said, startling Jackie and causing her to jump.

"Rachel! Is something wrong?" I asked.

"No, everything's fine," she replied. "Detective Shorts woke up."

"That's great," said Jackie.

"Your fiancé"—Rachel giggled with excitement about my engagement to Greg—"had to leave for work, so I've been keeping an eye one him. Imagine his surprise when he saw me sitting in the chair next to his bed."

Oh, I could just imagine. "We'll be by in a bit," I said, "but we're going to get some lunch first."

"OOO—Yums! You should pick up a turkey sandwich on rye," said Rachel.

"But you don't eat anything," Jackie said.

"Not for me!" Rachel huffed. "For the detective. Hospital food is disgusting and tastes bland. He needs real food if he's going to get his strength back."

Before I had a chance to respond, she vanished.

"We should go…" I began.

"Let's eat first," urged Jackie. "I'm starving."

I relented. Jackie had a point, and there wasn't much we could do at the hospital anyway. I headed back to town and decided to go to the sandwich shop that was on the same block as the Candle Shoppe. Actually, it was next door to the hobby store, but had the best sandwiches, which were always made with fresh-baked garlic bread. My mouth watered at the thought of biting into one of their subs.

"All, right," I said. "Lunch first."

Chapter 9

I should have known that the moment I had decided to go back to that little shopping strip that there would be trouble. I pulled up in front of the sandwich shop (which was only four stores down from the Candle Shoppe) to be inundated with police cars and their flashing lights once again. Officers walked around, taking notes and speaking to eye witnesses.

"You've got to be kidding me!" shrieked Jackie. "That's it. We need to find this person that is causing all of this trouble. It's bad enough that he broke into the place we work at, but mess with my favorite sandwich place and it's on!"

I chuckled a bit at Jackie's outburst. She loved her food, though I was getting tired of all these break-ins as well. I parked the car and we walked over and joined the crowd, listening in on the murmurings that took place. Judging from the way the police and the gathered crowd talked, nothing was taken from this place either. Why? Puzzled about the bizarre robberies, if you can even call them that since nothing was taken, I watched as the police questioned the store owner and any who might have seen something, but no one had. The break-in had taken place in the middle of night, long before anyone would have shown up for work.

"We should go," I said to Jackie.

"Hey, there's that psychic!" shouted one individual.

Oh no. This couldn't be good.

"Why didn't you warn us that this might happen?" he continued.

"It doesn't…" I began.

"Because she's a fake!" shouted another, "just like that article says."

"That's enough!" yelled one of the detectives I had seen in Mrs. Waverly's neighborhood. "There's nothing to see here, so you all can go about your business. You"—she pointed at me—"come here."

Great. So now I was in trouble again.

"Detective Nicole Henderson." She held out her hand and I took it. "Detective Shorts has warned me about you."

"He has?"

"Look, I don't know if you're the real deal and I don't care, but he has vouched for you, saying that you have been instrumental in helping him solve a few unsolvable cases."

I kept my mouth shut, not sure where she was going with this.

"Do you have any helpful information about these break-ins?"

"No," I said.

"Then why are you here?"

"Jackie and I were coming here for lunch. We usually stop here and get some sandwiches."

"You work at the Candle Shoppe, don't you?"

"Yes," I replied.

"According to the initial report, you were the one who first discovered the break-in."

"Yes."

"Have you been able to think of why anyone would want to break into the candle store."

"No."

"You were also the one that was involved in the shooting yesterday," said Detective Henderson.

"Detective Shorts saved me," I said. "He…"

"It's okay. I'm not accusing you of anything. My partner and I are now charged with this case, since Detective Shorts in in the hospital. If you can think of anything that you haven't already told the police, let me know." She handed me her card. "And you might want to be wary of the local newspaper."

She walked away, handing me another paper with a front page article about me, complete with a horrendous snapshot of me stuffing a piece of fried chicken in my mouth. Where did she get that picture? I showed it to Jackie. She grimaced and waved me to the car where who both sat and read the new article by Jillian Modsen.

Can't Even Save Her Friend

Jillian Modsen

A shooting took place near where the series of latest break-ins have occurred and none other than the supposed psychic Mellow Summers was involved. Being in tune with the spirit world, you would think that Miss Summers would have had an inkling that something like this might happen. One must question her abilities, since they failed to save a local detective from being injured. It was he who saved our resident psychic.

If Miss Summers is psychic, one must wonder why those around her are being harmed when she is in a position to warn them. People like her give true psychics a bad name. So, I urge Miss Summers to quit pretending, and tell the truth about her useless abilities.

Jackie slammed the paper down in her lap. "That little... She is smearing you, Mel! You should sue her for liable."

"I'm not sure if I can," I said. "Anyway, she has a point: those around me are getting hurt. Why can't I…"

"Because you aren't that kind of psychic. You're just a regular girl who happened to be the only one to speak to a ghost that needed help and you helped her. And ever since, ghosts seem to flock to you. That doesn't mean you can foresee the future. Good grief. Any idiot should know that psychics can't just predict the future upon command."

"I'll see if Tiny can get Calvin on the phone," I said. Calvin was a lawyer friend of Tiny's who helped me when the police had arrested me as the prime suspect in a murder investigation a couple of years ago. "We should head over to the hospital and see how Detective Shorts is doing."

Since we weren't going to be getting any sandwiches from our favorite little sandwich shop, we went straight to the hospital. As we walked into Detective Short's hospital room, I found Rachel, who stood in the center, tapping her foot with impatience.

"Well, it's about time," she said.

"Imagine my surprise," said Detective Shorts, though his voice sounded hoarse and he still looked pale, "when I woke up and found someone sitting there in that chair, only to have the same person vaporize into thin air."

I looked at Rachel.

"What?" she snapped at me. "You never said that I had to be visible the whole time. Fine. Can you see me now?"

Rachel materialized before everyone.

"Nope. Sorry. Can't," joked Jackie.

Rachel stomped her foot. "How about now?" She made herself as solid as she could and she looked like a real live person.

I glanced at Detective Shorts who arced an eyebrow at me. A metal pan clattered to the tile floor. We all jerked towards the noise. A nurse stood in the doorway (she had been bringing in a tray with Detective Shorts' lunch on it), except it now lay on the floor in a smeared mess, and a shocked expression was on her face.

"Gh-gh-ghost!"

"Oh, come on," said Rachel. "This is a hospital. A breeding ground for spooks and you work here. So, you should be used to it by now."

The nurse ran away, screaming.

"Do I have something in my teeth?" asked Rachel, opening her mouth wide so that we could all peer in it.

"I think it has something to do with you being an apparition," I said.

At that moment, Jillian Modsen walked in. Can't I ever get away from this lady?

"What do you want?" demanded Rachel in an irate, and unwelcoming, tone, loud enough for all to hear.

Jillian looked affronted and stepped back a moment because none of us had opened our mouths to speak and she couldn't see Rachel, who had decided to turn invisible again. Though, she had once explained that some people are so close-minded when it comes to the spirit world that they wouldn't ever see a ghost, even if one was right in front of them. Jillian struck me as one of those sorts of people.

"I was just coming to check on the good detective here," replied Jillian.

"Well, you're not welcome," spat Rachel.

I glared at her. Was she trying to give Jillian something else to write about?

"You mean that you were looking for a story," said Detective Shorts, his voice softer than normal.

"I was merely…" began Jillian.

"What is your problem?" I demanded of her, waving today's article in front of her. "You know I can sue you for this, right?"

"That gets to be a tricky area, Mellow," said Jillian. "I am just reporting the truth: that you are a self-proclaimed psychic who has failed to stop these break-ins, including the one that took place where you are currently employed, and failed to prevent the detective here from getting shot."

"I never made such claims," I said. "And these articles are ruining my reputation!"

"Pity," said Jillian.

"How would you like to have your personal ghost?" Rachel vaporized next to Jillian, but it appeared that I was the only one who saw her, or heard her. "Or your personal haunting?"

"I'm not concerned about your reputation, Mellow. Just the truth," said Jillian.

"The truth?" said Jackie. "More like your version of it. You don't believe in anything paranormal—"

"She will when I'm through with her," Rachel interjected.

"—and so you plan to destroy someone who is of that persuasion," finished Jackie, not hearing Rachel.

"Ghosts are not real," said Jillian.

"You want to make a bet?" said Rachel.

"People like you," continued Jillian, unaware that Rachel had spoken, "prey upon those so desperate to hear from the other side. I watched as my mother succumbed to such madness. Shoveling out hundreds to even thousands of dollars just so she could hear my father speak again. She went bankrupt. I intend to expose the frauds for what they are."

"Mel, is no fraud," said Jackie.

"You're her friend," said Jillian, "of course you would say such things."

"So am I." Rachel pushed Jillian, but remained invisible.

"Miss Modsen," said Detective Shorts, his croaky voice stopping our confrontation, "you are not welcome here. I have nothing to say to you, nor do I have a statement that I wish to give. Miss Summers and her friends were invited here. You were not."

"Very well," said Jillian, taking her cue to leave.

"And you can take this trash with you," said Jackie, yanking the paper from my hand and shoving it into Jillian's.

"How about I make her eat it?" said Rachel, but I shook my head at her. "I can do it when you're not looking."

"And next time you do not like something I write," said Jillian before she walked through the door, "don't ram bananas, or whatever that was, up my tailpipe. Or put sugar in the gas tank."

"It was snow you idiot," said Rachel in a huff with her arms crossed.

"You put sugar in her gas tank?" asked Detective Shorts, after Jillian had left.

"I think you'll find that it was…"

"Me!" Rachel made herself visible for us all to see. "Totally me. I should key her car next. That's an awesome idea!"

"Rachel…" I said, trying to stop her, but she vanished before I could finish my sentence. "And she's gone. Again."

"We really shouldn't allow her to do that," said Detective Shorts.

"You're welcome to try and arrest her," I replied.

He laughed a little at that remark.

"How are you feeling?" asked Jackie.

"Sore," he replied, "but I'll live. You, on the other hand, I am more worried about." Detective Shorts looked at me.

"You don't need to worry about me," I said.

"Sure he doesn't" scoffed Jackie.

"How far are you in your investigation of the break-ins?" asked Detective Shorts.

"Investigation?" I tried to play innocent, but he saw right through me and gave me that look of his that says he knows I'm lying.

"You already know that the flower shop had been broken into, but so has the hobby store and the…"

"Sandwich shop," said Jackie. "Now I can't have my BLT with mustard sauce."

"The old photography studio," mumbled the detective, more to himself than to us.

"That's what that lady, what was her name, Beverly Waverly said," Jackie said.

"Waverly?" Detective Shorts' tone changed from curious to very interested.

"Yes," said Jackie.

"What were you doing in Hildegard Heights?" asked Detective Shorts.

"Looking for the black sedan that the shooter used," I replied.

Despite the fact that Detective Shorts was hooked

up to an IV and wearing the typical hospital gown that did little to cover anything, he still managed to give me a glare that made me quiver; Jackie too. We shrank beneath his reprimanding gaze. "Without backup?"

"Greg was here, keeping an eye on you, but he had to go to work, so Rachel took over."

"Sometimes I wish I had never met you," Detective Shorts said.

I looked away, not sure of how to respond.

"Before you, I never once believed that I was under the watchful eyes of a ghost. And my life was much less interesting."

"You were saying the same thing about..." started Jackie, but she stopped herself. "Never mind."

"The matching sedan was at a house up the street from Mrs. Waverly and the owner was arrested by a Detective Nicole Henderson."

"Yes, she transferred in last month from the Los Angeles area," said Detective Shorts.

"Who's Roger?" I asked, remembering the name that Beverly Waverly had mentioned.

Detective Shorts frowned. "I shouldn't tell you because you will just go off on your own to investigate. However, I know that if I don't tell you, you will go off on your own anyway to learn the truth. Roger Croukman. He was accused of murdering his fiancé the night before their wedding. The jury had decided that the evidence was enough to convict him and gave a verdict of guilty. I haven't thought of him in over 20 years. I was just an officer then and had only been on the force for a few years, but I remember being one of the first officers on the scene.

"Roger claimed he was innocent, but all of the eye-witness testimony placed him at the scene and he was the last known person to see his fiancé alive. The Candle Shoppe, the Flower Boutique, hobby store, and the deli, there, were all once part of a photo studio that had taken up that entire strip. Of course, it was 20 years ago. As luck would have it, the man who owned it died the same night that Roger murdered his fiancé. Struck by lightning. The fool loved to film lightning and there was quite a storm that night. He went out into a field with his camera to catch some amazing photography, but he got a little more than he bargained for and was pronounced dead on arrival. Sometime later, his estate sold off the studio and it later became the four little stores that are there now."

"So that's why you were a bit evasive yesterday," I said.

"I didn't think much about the Candle Shoppe being broken into, but when the flower store was also treated in the same manner, I started to wonder if maybe this was connected. So, I went into the old case files and pulled out anything pertaining to Roger and his fiancé's murder. He always maintained his innocence. He was released from the state penitentiary two weeks ago. Served his full time in prison. Sentenced to 20 years and he served the full 20."

"So he did it," said Jackie.

"Not necessarily," said Detective Shorts. "I thought so too, but though he couldn't provide an alibi for the first break-in, he had one for the second occurrence."

"Well, all four were broken into," said Jackie, "so that means that if the perpetrator didn't find what he wants, he won't be back."

"I think," replied Detective Shorts, "that he might. These are not your typical break-ins. Nothing was stolen, nothing valuable anyway. The person might come back, but later, when things settle."

"Unless we set a trap," I said.

"No," both Jackie and Detective Shorts said at the same time.

"Mel, the last time we did something like that, you almost got hurt," said Jackie.

"I agree," said Detective Shorts. "Under no circumstance are you to set up a trap with yourself as bait."

"Fine," I said.

"I mean it, Miss Summers," said the detective.

"I promise not to use myself as bait," I said.

"Excuse me," said a middle-aged woman in a nurse's outfit, "but I'm going to have to ask you two to leave. One of my nurses is screaming about ghosts and…"

"I did it!" Rachel appeared in the middle of the room, screaming at the top of her lungs.

The head nurse looked at her, her eyes growing wide, and fainted.

"I think she's been working too hard," said Rachel.

"We need to go," I told her.

"Be careful, Miss Summers," Detective Shorts called after me.

"Hey, don't worry," said Rachel. "She's got me!"

Chapter 10

"So where to now?" asked Jackie as we left the hospital.

"We need some information," I said.

"Jack?" asked Jackie.

"Jack," I replied.

Jackie frowned. I understood why. The last time we had gone to see Jack, he was not too pleased to see us. In fact, he had said maybe five words and did not bother to look up from his computer screen, treating us as though we were more of an annoyance than friends. Though, I'm not sure if Jack ever considered us friends. He was Greg's cousin and we usually used him more for his ability to get information than anything else, something that we might want to think about changing.

I pulled out my phone and dialed Greg.

"Mel?"

"Hey," I said. "We need to go to Jack and have him look up some leads for us. Is there any way you can meet us there?"

"I get off in about an hour," said Greg. "I'll see you then."

"Okay. Bye."

"So?" asked Jackie.

"He'll meet us down there in an hour."

"Good. Then, we still have time to get some lunch."

While we waited for Greg to get off work, Jackie and I went to a local diner for lunch. The small restaurant had one of those long counters that stretched around the kitchen in a u-shape bend with small, red chairs, that twisted and turned, surrounding it. The compact dining space did not detract from its popularity. We managed to squeeze in and find two seats at the counter. We ran to them, plopping our behinds on the cushions before two construction workers, who had the same idea, could.

"Hey!" said one. "Ouch!" He rubbed the back of his head where a salt shaker, thrown by—you guessed it—Rachel had hit him.

"Find your own seats!" she yelled at them.

They walked off, thinking that some other customer had shouted at them.

Jackie and I took our seats and two menus floated across the counter into our hands. We seized them before anyone could see the menus hovering in midair.

"I'm thinking of the grilled cheese," said Jackie.

"No, that's fattening," commented Rachel. "All that cheese."

"Then there's the tomato soup," mused Jackie.

"I think it just comes from a can," Rachel said. "It's going to have that metallic taste."

"Hey," I said, pointing at the menu, "this hamburger sounds good."

"But it doesn't have any bacon," Rachel continued to voice her opinion on our food choices. "I'm sure it costs extra."

"Rachel," I said to her, "please."

"Sorry," said Rachel. "It's not often I get to be in an eatery. Besides, you two should really eat more salads."

"I thought you wanted her to eat bacon," Jackie said to Rachel, while trying to look as though she talked to me. "That's not exactly healthy."

"Bacon is healthy no matter what time of day it is. And it is an essential part of any well-rounded diet. It's bacon. Bacon means delicious!" Rachel sang that last word, garnering a few odd glances.

"Are you ready to order?" asked the waitress.

Jackie ordered the grilled cheese sandwich, despite Rachel making gag-faces at her and pretending to throw up, and I requested the hamburger with fries.

"I told you," said Rachel when the waitress left, "you need to eat more salad."

"It's a diner," I whispered to her. "I don't think they even have the makings for a salad."

"Sure they do," said Rachel. "I'll prove it to you." She vanished.

While she was gone, our food arrived and both Jackie and I tore into our meals, acting as though we hadn't eaten in days, even though it had only been since that morning. I had just finished the last bite of my burger when I heard a familiar voice."

"Mellow, isn't it?"

I turned. Detective Henderson had walked into the diner with her partner and both looked at Jackie and me, me with my ketchup and mustard stained face while Jackie sported a mixture of cheese and bread crumbs on hers. We both snatched out napkins and wiped our mouths.

"Can I help you, detective?" I asked. Was she following me? Something told me that this accidental meeting had not been coincidental.

The detective took a seat next to me. "It has come to my attention that your name is on the list of approved visitors to Hildegarde Heights, put there by a Beverly Waverly."

Well I'll be. Beverly did put me on her visitors' list. "We"—I pointed at Jackie and myself—"saw her this morning."

"Oh. Have you known her long?" asked the detective.

Nope. This meeting definitely was not a coincidence. "Only since this morning," I said.

"Interesting," said Detective Henderson.

"What is this all about?" I asked.

"I tried to speak with her today, but she clammed up. It seems that she is not fond of the police, especially the local police."

"And you want me to talk to her."

"I am asking for your help," said the detective. "I just want to know more about this Roger Croukman and a case that happened 20 years ago. I believe that it might have something to do with why someone made an attempt on Detective Shorts' life."

"I'm not sure she'll talk to me about it," I said.

"Just be her friend and if the conversation should get steered toward what happened 20 years ago, just listen and…"

"I'm not wearing a wire," I said.

"Fine. Just let me know if she says anything pertinent to yesterday's shooting."

"I'll think about it," I said.

"Do that."

"Hey!" All eyes turned in the direction of Rachel's voice; she stood in the doorway to the kitchen, the doors swinging back and forth making *fwap-fwap* sounds, holding up a head of iceberg lettuce and a tomato. "They do have the fixings for a salad!"

The bustling noise of clanging pans, clinking forks, and lively conversation ceased; it was so silent that even a pin failed to make the slightest noise. Rachel eyed the crowd before her, realizing that she had been louder than she had planned, and watched the blank stares from people who had stopped eating just to gawk at her. A man next to us held his fork in front of him; the piece of pie on it fell to the mosaic tile of the counter, decorating it's white color with a splash of cinnamon and sugar.

Taking our cue to leave, Jackie and I stood up, dumped some cash on the counter to pay our check, and walked out of the swinging glass doors. No one bothered to stop us, their eyes still glued to the hovering head of lettuce and tomato.

Rachel walked over to Detective Henderson—all the customers saw was two floating vegetables that had fixated on one individual—while those near her hurried away as though touching the lettuce and tomato meant certain death. The detective said nothing, and managed to keep a straight face, as the floating lettuce and tomato settled in her hands.

"Here," said Rachel, "you look like you could use these."

Detective Henderson's eyes widened, but she remained calm.

Once outside, we all piled into my car and drove to the police station to meet up with Greg as the hour we had needed to kill was up.

I pulled into the parking lot—boy was it crowded!—at the police department, winding my way through the narrow rows and the parked cars that formed a lopsided line with bumps and uneven, reflective edges. A space opened up. Not caring who I would have to cut off to get it, I sped up and pulled in just as another car thought he could do the same. Maddening honks and a string of cuss words filled the air as the driver made his displeasure known.

"Oh, no he didn't," said Rachel when the man referred to me as something that came out of the back end of an elephant. She vanished from the back seat, appeared in front of his car, and slammed her fists on the rusty hood, screaming, "We were here first! Get your own space!"

Rachel disappeared before the man's eyes. As we got out of the car and walked over to the lobby entrance, the man sat frozen, rooted to his car seat, unable to move. In response, Rachel materialized next to his car window. "Hey," she said to him, jerking him back to reality, "you're blocking traffic."

When she vanished again, only to show up by my side, the man gunned his engine, tires squealing, as he tore out of the parking lot and hurried far away from us, with Rachel chortling.

"That was so much fun!" she said.

I kept my mouth shut. There was no point in raining

on her parade, and the man did bring it upon himself, though maybe I shouldn't have been in such a hurry to get a parking space.

Greg waited for us by the glass doors as we walked up; Rachel skipped like a schoolgirl, pleased with herself and her antics at the diner, as well as the parking lot. "We don't have much time," said Greg, opening the door and ushering us inside. Rachel had disappeared again.

"What's wrong?" I asked.

"Jack is under a lot of pressure right now. The new detective that transferred here somehow got wind that he has been helping us, or digging into files without permission. Though he is not officially under investigation, she is keeping a close eye on him."

"Maybe we should go," I said.

"No." Greg led us down the stairs and into the basement where Jack's office was. "He's already promised to look into the old case files concerning that 20-year-old murder you told me about, but we need to be quick."

Doing our best to not attract attention, we hurried down the stairwell and through the hallway that led to Jack's office, piling in there and shutting the door.

"It's about time," said Jack. "That Detective Henderson just phoned me, asking me questions about you."

"Really?" asked Greg.

"Well, not directly, but she seems to know something and I don't want to get into trouble."

I guess this explained why he had been rude to Jackie and me when we stopped by the day before.

"So never again after this," said Jack.

Greg said nothing, but got one of those all-knowing looks on his face that said he didn't believe Jack's stance. I knew Greg. He always had a way to get his cousin to do things.

"I just need to know about a murder that took place 20 years ago. The man convicted was named Roger Croukman."

Jack turned toward his computer and punched the keys at lightning speed, bringing up screen after screen until…

"Here," he said. "I remember this one. It was one of the most publicized cases in this area, garnering a lot of attention. Some people are still upset about it, thinking that the guy should have gotten the chair."

"Can you print it off?" I asked.

"Some of the case files are locked and have been redacted, but I can get you a few photos that were used in the trial."

"What happened, anyway?" asked Jackie.

I looked around for Rachel, wondering where she had gone off to. She could be so unpredictable.

Jack leaned closer to the screen so he could read the small print. "Back in 1995 there was a huge murder trial, well, huge for this area, that took place. Roger Croukman and his fiancé were about to get married. They were essentially the couple of the century in this city and their marriage was a huge affair. The night before their wedding, they had a huge party—the pre-wedding dinner. Just about everyone was invited, but it seems that not everything was going well.

"Roger's fiancé, Brianna, was last seen going into the gazebo with him. They talked and witnesses said that it got a little heated. Roger was last seen leaving the gazebo and re-joined the party, though no one saw him the rest of the night. About an hour later, Brianna was found dead.

"Since no one could find Roger at first, the police feared that he might have been a victim as well, but when they found him unharmed in his room, their theory changed. Soon after, the evidence against him piled up. Eyewitnesses said he was the last to see Brianna alive. No one else was seen entering or leaving the gazebo. Photos place him there, and they are time stamped, making it difficult to argue against it."

"All of this is circumstantial," I said. "Just because no one saw another person enter the gazebo, doesn't mean that there wasn't one."

"True," replied Jack, "but there is no proof to back it up. Roger always maintained his innocence, even while in prison. He said that the photographer could prove he didn't do; the only problem is, the guy is dead."

I frowned, remembering that Detective Shorts had said that the photographer died that night from being struck by lightning.

"Them's the breaks, huh?" said Jackie. "To have the only person who can prove your innocence die. Talk about cruel."

"That's assuming he is innocent," said Greg.

"So how does this play into the break-ins?" asked Jackie.

The printer hummed and printed off several photos that had been used in the trial. I grabbed them and flipped through them, stopping on one in particular.

"I think I know." I handed the photograph to Jackie. "Doesn't he look familiar?"

She took the picture and gasped. In it was the image of the man we had seen at various times since we started working at the Candle Shoppe. He held his camera, taking pictures of the guests, but in this instance, the people stood in front of a mirror and his reflection showed up.

"Him?" asked Jackie.

I shook my head, not believing that I never realized he was a spirit still wandering this earth, though, he had never made any indication that he was one.

"What?" asked Greg, taking the picture.

"We've seen him before," I said. "He's been one of our regulars at the Candle Shoppe, always coming in and leaving. Though, we never did see him come in through the front door."

"Or leave," said Jackie. "And when we did see him, it was usually during a time when we had a lot of customers."

"I know where we're headed next," Greg said.

"Yeah, well," interrupted Jack, "you might want to head over to Beverly Waverly's place."

"Why?" asked Greg.

"According to the trial transcripts," answered Jack, "she was the only person who believed Roger's story and even testified that she didn't think he had done it."

Well, that explained why Detective Henderson wanted me to speak with Mrs. Waverly. She also thought that the two incidents were connected (the break-ins and Roger's conviction) and probably believed that since Mrs. Waverly had put me on her guest list, I would be in a perfect position to talk with her. The thing was, I needed to talk to her now.

"I guess we'll need Rachel to find the photographer's spirit," said Jackie. "Where is she anyway?"

"I don't know," I said. "I haven't seen her since the parking lot." The fact that Rachel had disappeared like that didn't bode well and I had a feeling that she was up to something.

Hurried steps sounded outside the door, growing louder until they passed and faded.

"We should go," said Greg.

"About that other matter," said Jack, making us stop.

I glanced around for any sign that Rachel had shown up, but found none.

"What other matter?" asked Jackie.

That's right! I had forgotten to tell her. "Tell you later," I whispered.

Jack yanked open a drawer in his desk and pulled out an envelope, handing it to me. "This everything I could find on that guy you and Greg had me look up. I'm sorry, but there was nothing else I could find."

"Thanks," I told him.

We left Jack's office, peeking around the door to make sure that a certain detective was not watching and made our way outside.

"Now," said Jackie when we got out into the cold air. "What's this all about."

I pulled her close and leaned in just in case Rachel showed up. "I asked Greg to have Jack look up the information for Tom's current whereabouts, Rachel's fiancé."

"What?"

"She was feeling down during my engagement party

and I remembered that she had been engaged when she was murdered. I just thought that maybe I could help her get a little bit of closure."

"Why didn't you tell me?" asked Jackie.

"I… uh… forgot."

Jackie glared at me with a "how could you" look, which made me feel even worse, but before I had a chance to apologize to her, Jillian showed up. What was it with this woman? Was she stalking me? Everywhere I went, she appeared.

"Well," she said in a snide tone, "if it isn't the *Apple Dumpling Gang*."

"Jillian," Jackie returned her snide tone and fake smile, "how unpleasant it is to see you."

Jillian smirked, unimpressed by Jackie's retort. "So what is a psychic doing here at the police station? Don't tell me they arrested you for fraud."

"Don't you wish," spat Jackie.

"What do you want?" I said, holding Jackie back.

"Nothing," replied Jillian.

Greg snorted in disbelief. "You're a reporter. I doubt that you are up to just nothing. Leave my fiancé alone."

"Fiancé?" said Jillian, her eyes lit up and I knew she had just gotten another idea for an article about me.

Greg must have sensed it too because his face looked as though he wished he could take back his words. "Why don't you make your career by doing something honest?"

"Telling the truth is always honest," said Jillian.

"Except when it's one-sided," muttered Jackie.

A water bottle appeared above her head and I knew who had done it, even though she remained invisible: Rachel. I watched as the water bottle tipped upside down, dumping its contents all over Jillian and her coat and silk blouse.

"What?" she screamed. "My blouse!" She jumped around, shaking the water from her shirt, her hair dripping, sending streams of water down her face. "You!" she spat at me.

Before I had a chance to say anything, her car, which had been parallel-parked on the curb, moved.

"Your car's moving!" shouted Rachel.

Jillian turned, forgetting her waterlogged blouse and wet hairdo. Her mouth dropped as she watched her car roll downhill, heading straight for a hot dog stand. "My car!"

Jillian ran towards her car, her heels clicking on the pavement—it was a wonder she didn't slip and fall on the ice—waving her arms, her bag bumping against her side. She never made it. Her car smashed into the hot dog stand amid shouts and screams of terror, rolling over it before it was stopped by a fire hydrant. Curses flowed from her red-painted lips as she thrashed about in the street.

"E-brakes are so overrated," said Rachel with a giggle.

"Rachel, did you have to…" I began.

"Yes, I did." She vanished.

Chapter 11

"I think we need to see Mrs. Waverly again," I said."

"Again?" asked Greg, and I remembered that I hadn't told him about how Jackie and I had run into her earlier that day.

"Right now?" asked Jackie.

"Yes," I replied. "Besides, I have a feeling that Detective Henderson will be asking me about it soon anyway. And after what we've learned about some murder, where she insisted that the convicted individual was innocent, I think we should take her up on her offer for a visit."

Jackie huffed.

"I'll buy you some tacos later on," I said.

"Double stuffed with extra cheese?" asked Jackie.

"And hot sauce," I said.

"Let's go."

I got into Greg's car, while Jackie followed us in mine, and we drove to Hildegard Heights for the second time today, except this time I was on the guest list.

"What's your business here?" demanded the guard as we pulled up to the gate.

"My name is Mellow Summers," I said, leaning across Greg so that I could talk to the guard. "Mrs. Beverly Waverly said that she had me put on the guest list."

The guard's face scrunched up in a disapproving look and I would have sworn that it resembled as baby squirrel's skin more than a human face. He got out his tablet with the list of approved visitors and scrolled through the screen, his frown deepening with each passing second, until he stopped. "So, it seems that you are telling the truth."

He stepped back into the little guardhouse and pulled a lever, opening the gate and allowing us through. Greg drove through the street, which formed a circle, to the house, with me directing him. As we passed the snowbank that I had plowed into, I glanced at Jackie; she gave me a knowing look, but said nothing, for which I was thankful.

"There's her house," I said.

Greg nodded and parked on the side of the road, avoiding the piles of snow better than I had earlier that morning.

As we walked up the curving sidewalk, which had been cleared of snow and was remarkably dry, I noticed the gardener, Donald, watching us, and he was none too pleased to see me or Jackie again; and I think the fact that we had brought Greg infuriated him as well. I knocked on the oak door and saw a shape approach through the diamond-shaped window.

"Yes?"

"Mrs. Waverly?" I said. "It's me, Mellow. I'm sorry I didn't call, but you said I could visit at any time."

"Oh, yes, dear, come in." She opened the door wider. "And please call me Beverly. Mrs. Waverly makes me sound so old."

"Thank you." I stepped into the foyer and couldn't believe that I was able to see my reflection in the floor. "I hope you don't mind that I brought a couple of friends. You remember Jackie from this morning and this is Greg. We just got engaged."

I held up my ring finger and wiggled it at her. Beverly's face lit up when she saw it and she placed her slender hands over her mouth as though she was trying to keep from crying out in joy.

"Oh, congratulations the both of you," she said.

She led us through the foyer and into a sitting area, walking us past a mirror, which allowed me to see just how frazzled my long hair had gotten from the day's events. Her sitting room made our mouths hang open. Instead of the normal wood chairs with thin cushions that hurt your bottom after a few minutes of sitting on them, plush couches that you sunk into and over-sized easy chairs with cushions so soft that they swallowed you filled the open room. We each picked a place to sit and my butt thanked me for remembering that it needed some luxury too as I eased into one of the oversized chairs, marveling at how comfortable it was, running my fingers along the soft, velvety material.

Beverly chuckled as she watched our faces go from unsure to pure bliss. "These are comfortable, aren't they?"

I'll say. They were luxurious. I found myself wishing I could take one of the chairs home with me and one glance at both Jackie and Greg told me that I wasn't alone.

"Now, dear," said Beverly, "why don't you tell me why you are here?"

I thought about lying and telling her that I had come for a simple visit, but it was clear that she knew I was there for something else. So, I decided that honesty would be the best policy. "Well," I said, "truthfully, I came to talk about Roger and his fiancé, Brianna."

"Is he in trouble?" Beverly's face grew concerned and I was afraid that I might have upset her.

"No," I said, "it's just I'm working on something…"

"I thought you might be," said Beverly.

"I think it might be connected to what happened 20 years ago," I finished.

A crunch distracted me. I looked over at Jackie as she tried to brush crumbs from her chin and hide the cookie in her hand, which she had discovered on the tiered serving plates on the coffee table.

"Do help yourselves," Beverly said, waving away any possibility of embarrassment. "The cook makes them, but I can't eat them all."

Jackie's face relaxed and she took another bite of her lemon cookie.

"What happened 20 years ago is a tragedy and not just because poor Brianna died, but because an innocent man went to prison."

"But according to the police report, and the eyewitness testimony at the trial, he was there when it happened," said Greg.

"So were a lot of other people," replied Beverly.

"Mrs.—Beverly," I broke in, "of all the people present at the time, you were the only one who believed Roger's story. Why?"

"Because my mother has always had a soft spot where Roger's concerned," said a strong voice, forcing us all to turn and face him.

"Edmond." Beverly stood up and hugged her son. "When did you get into town?"

"A few days ago," replied Edmond. "I'm sorry that I didn't come by sooner. I had a few things to clear up."

"Oh, where are my manners?" said Beverly when Edmond looked at me. "This is Mellow—our resident psychic, you know—her friend Jackie, and her new fiancé Greg."

"Nice to meet you all." Edmond paused when he shook my hand. "You are the one I've been reading about in the paper."

"Look, I'm no psychic," I said, feeling embarrassed. "It doesn't work like that."

"You've nothing to fear here," said Edmond. "We don't believe much of what is in the paper these days."

"Edmond lives in New York City," said Beverly. "I don't get to see him as much as I'd like and wish he'd visit more often."

"I'm here now and intend to stay here for the next several days. Now, you were asking about Roger?"

"Mostly about what happened 20 years ago," I said.

"Is there a particular reason you are interested?" asked Edmond.

"I don't really want to go into it," I replied. "I just

think that it might be connected to something I am looking into right now."

"Ah, so the rumors about you being a private investigator are true," Edmond said with a pleasant smile.

I chose not to reply. I had never referred to myself as a private investigator, but if he wanted to think I was one, maybe it would work in my favor.

"Well," said Edmond, "you'll find nothing but help here. Roger and I were good friends through most of school. We even went to college together, and though I pursued a career on wall street and he chose to have a much smaller enterprise in business, we remained good friends. Roger met Brianna our second year of college and they soon fell in love. It turned out that she was from a prominent family the next town over. What are the odds?

"After graduation, they decided to have their wedding that summer and their wedding was the talk of the town. It is unfortunate that the dinner the night before the wedding—well, party would describe it better—ended the way it did."

"What happened, exactly?" asked Jackie through a mouthful of cookies.

"Roger and Brianna had an argument. I'm not sure what about, but it caused her to storm away from the party. Roger followed her and they went into the gazebo that was outside the hotel. People saw Roger leave alone, but no one saw Brianna again that night. The police believed that she had been dead a good three hours before anyone noticed she had been missing."

"And since Roger was the last one to be seen with her while she was alive, he became the prime suspect," said Greg.

"Yes," said Edmond.

"But he didn't do it," said Beverly.

"Mom," said Edmond, "I know you want to believe that, but the evidence said otherwise."

"The evidence is all circumstantial," said Beverly.

"But the jury…" began Edmond.

"Made a mistake," said Beverly. "I know it might sound like a typical response coming from an old lady, but Roger could never have harmed Brianna. Someone else must have."

"Ma'am," said a server as he walked in, "your appointment is here."

"Thank you, Jeffry," said Beverly. "I am sorry, but I'm afraid I have to cut this short."

"That's all right," I said. "It is getting late and we should be going anyway. Thank you."

"And thanks for the cookies," said Jackie, brushing crumbs off her lap.

"I hope I've been able to help you," said Beverly, "and don't hesitate to call me." She turned to a table with a pen and pad of paper on it, wrote down her number, and handed it to me. "It's my cell."

"Thank you," I said. "Have a good evening."

Edmond walked us out. "And as my mother said, don't hesitate to call if you need anything."

I smiled and walked back to the car with Greg and Jackie.

Chapter 12

I had to get to the Candle Shoppe. That was where all of this had begun. Ever since I had walked in and discovered that it had been broken into, my life had gone in a tailspin with a reporter smearing my name and reputation to make her career; Detective Shorts ending up in the hospital after getting shot; and four businesses in total have been broken into, but with nothing taken.

"Where to now?" asked Jackie.

"The Candle Shoppe," I replied. It was late afternoon and I knew that the sun would be setting soon. Perhaps we could break in after dark.

"I knew you were going to want to go there," Jackie replied.

"I still have the key." I held up the store key and waved it in front of both her and Greg.

"All right, let's go," said Jackie.

Pleased, I skipped a bit as we walked to our cars. Greg had decided that he would follow Jackie and me to the Candle Shoppe. For the first time all week, I pulled up to the small shopping area and there weren't any police cars around; just the normal bustle of those who spend their time window shopping or going in and out of stores with packages under their arms.

I parked down the street from the Candle Shoppe and Greg pulled into a space beside me. We hurried to the empty alley where the back door was and I took out the key, ramming it into the dented lock, and let us inside. Though Mr. Stilton had tried cleaning up some on his own, there were still items all over the floor and what had been cleared to form a walking path, lay in a jumbled mess on the desk and chairs.

I looked around, wondering where to start, since I had no idea what the perpetrator would want—no point in calling him a thief since he didn't take anything. As I scanned the wall and the chipped wood and dust that littered the floor along the floorboards, a dark space caught my attention. The hole in the wall. I smacked myself for being so forgetful. When I had first found the Candle Shoppe like this, I had also discovered a hole in the wall, but without a flashlight I wasn't able to get a good look inside.

"You shouldn't be here as you haven't permission," said a voice.

We all turned and gasped when we saw the man, whom Jackie and I had always thought was a customer, standing in front of us.

"Only authorized personnel are allowed in this place,"

said the ghost without looking at us; I don't think he saw us in the sense that we think of being seen, as his eyes seemed to look past us.

"We're sorry," I said.

"All clients belong in the studio, but you must go"—he pointed at Greg—"because we can only have a duo."

"Excuse me?" I said, but the ghost disappeared.

We stared at the place he had been, confused about his quip about the studio and only duos being allowed.

"What the heck was that all about?" asked Jackie.

"I don't know," I said, "but we need Rachel. Rachel? Rachel!"

No answer. Figures. She always showed up when I least expected it, or wished she wouldn't; but when I needed her, that as when she decided to play hooky.

"RACHEL!" I shouted, startling both Greg and Jackie.

"What?" said Rachel, appearing before me in a seated position on the desk. "You shout so loud that even the dead can hear you."

"I think that was the idea," muttered Greg, garnering a glare from Rachel.

"We saw a ghost," I said.

"Congratulations," Rachel replied. "I should think you would be used to that by now."

"No, you don't understand. He seems to be one that has been haunting this place for a while, but I'm wondering if he even knows that he is dead. In either case, when he does show up, he speaks in riddles."

"Oh!" said Rachel, leaning forward. "Why didn't you say so. Where is he?"

"He just vanished," I replied. "I don't know where he is, but I was wondering if you could…"

"Say no more," Rachel held up her hand, stopping me. "I'll find him." She popped out of the room.

I led Jackie and Greg to the hole in the wall, pointing it out to them. They agreed that it made no sense to knock a hole in the wall, since it was mostly hollow on the inside with just a few bits of pink insulation filling its interior. I reached into my purse for my flashlight and cursed for not remembering to stick it in there. That was the second time I had forgotten to bring it with me.

Seeing my frustration, Greg found a floor lamp, unplugged it, and brought it over, plugging it into the wall and taking the shade off so that the bulb was exposed. He stuck it in the hole and I poked my head inside, looking around as best I could. Even with the light, I didn't find anything of interest, nothing that would tell me why someone would knock a hole in the wall. There was no hidden safe or compartment.

"I still don't get it," I said.

Greg poked his head in the hole while I held the lamp, looking side to side and up and down. "Well," he said, "there would be no reason for someone who was interested in finding something that was hidden 20 years ago to be looking in this wall."

"Why?" I asked.

"The wall itself is only ten years old," replied Greg.

"How do you know?" asked Jackie.

"Well," said Greg, pulling his head out of the hole, "for starters, the construction of the beams are different. They didn't build them like this in the 90s. Building codes have changed a little since then. Also, on the support beam here"—he smacked the wall with his fist, indicating which beam he referred to—"has the date of March 13, 2005 written on it. There also isn't much sign of rot on it. Over time wood used in construction will decay and rot; it's inevitable, hence why reconstruction is done. These are fairly new."

"How do you know all this?" asked Jackie.

"I used to work construction," said Greg. "Did that right after high school until I settled into my more regular job and met someone remarkable." He pulled me close and gave me a kiss.

"Oh, quit the mushy stuff," said Jackie, turning away.

"Sorry," I apologized. I did try to keep such things to a minimum around people and public places. Some things are better done in private.

"You know, you still owe me some tacos," said Jackie.

"Now?" I asked.

"Problem solved!" Rachel burst into the room with a bag of tacos, from a little pace called *Munchies*, in one hand and a ghost on her other arm: the one that we had been seeing for the last few years and never realized he was a spirit.

"How did you…" I began.

"I overheard you make the deal with Jackie," replied Rachel. "Don't worry, I paid for them with the money I took from your wallet."

What? I ripped open my purse, yanking out my wallet, and opening it. Yep, more cash was gone. "We really need to talk about this whole taking money out of my purse thing."

Rachel lowered her head with a guilty expression on her face.

Leaving the wallet issue alone for a while, I turned to the man that Rachel had brought with her, our ghostly visitor that neither Jackie nor I knew we had. "What do I call you?"

"My name is that of a craftsman of many trades, working for lords and ladies of London's noble days. From lowly birth to royal appointment."

"Uh... what?" asked Greg, just as confused as I was.

"Yeah, he's been talking like that since I found him. This guy's a loon!" Rachel shook him. "Wake up! You're dead."

"What's wrong with him?" I asked.

"Not sure exactly," replied Rachel, "but he is in what we in the spirit world call a ghostly stupor."

"Ghostly stupor?" said Greg.

"Yeah. Sometimes people do not know that they are dead and so they wander the earth much like they did while alive. My guess is that he has no idea that he died."

Makes sense. I had heard stories about residual hauntings that were just echoes of what happened in the past, but I had also read stories about hauntings where the ghosts had no idea they were doing the haunting. Sometimes, when a person died a sudden death, they didn't realize that they had died, so they go back to a place that was familiar to them in life, and probably even saw it the way it was when they had lived. Maybe that was case with him. But why the riddles? Could it have been a quirk of his while he was still alive.

"Gregory King!" shouted Jackie through a mouthful of tacos. She had already eaten two of them and had the wrappers scrunched in her hand while she worked on her third taco.

"Who?" asked Greg.

"There was a man who lived in England in the 17th century. He was born to a lower class family, but worked as an engraver and a surveyor. Eventually, he moved to London and was later appointed Secretary to the Commission of Public Accounts and Secretary to the Controllers of Army Accounts. His name was Gregory King."

"How do you know all of this?" I asked, surprised by her knowledge, since he wasn't a major figure in history.

"The History Channel had a special on him while you and Greg were away for the weekend," replied Jackie. "Maybe it's his name too. Sometimes people do share names of someone in history, even if they aren't related."

"Mr. King," I said, approaching the man. "Mr. Gregory King?"

He got a look of recognition on his face and, for a moment, I thought that he had come back to the present.

"Of King's Photography and Studio," he said. "this is my place."

I remembered how Jack had mentioned that this entire block of shops had been a photography studio.

"What has happened to my office?" said Gregory, the ghost.

"Mr. King," I said, keeping my voice calm and gentle, trying to not scare him away, "do you remember the party—the pre-wedding dinner of Roger and Brianna."

"A charming couple," said Gregory. "Moments of life I captured for all posterity and their ever after."

Okay, so we are back to the riddles and rhymes. "You mean, you took their pictures."

"Yes," said Gregory. "I was their wedding photographer."

And back to somewhat coherent. "Can you remember anything strange about that night?"

"Rage and jitters filled the air, tearing poor couple a snare."

"You mean that Roger and Brianna had a fight," I said.

"Miniscule in measure, but enough to interrupt their pleasure."

"Do you know what they argued about?"

"No. In the distance I remained, capturing life's little games. But alone Brianna was not, for another feared being caught."

"Wait a minute," said Greg, "the police were convinced that Roger was the last person to see her alive."

"Was there another who met with Brianna?" I asked.

"Two there were: one her groom and one her doom." Gregory King started to fade and I feared that we were losing him. What if he had witnessed the murder of Brianna and knew who the real murderer was? That would mean that Beverly was correct in her conviction of Roger Croukman's innocence. But how would I prove it? A ghost cannot make a statement to the police or take the witness stand.

"Mr. King," I said, "did you see what happened? Did you see Brianna's murder?"

I had pushed it too far. Gregory's ghost looked right at me, an irate expression on his face and faded to the point where I could only see a faint outline, but no distinguishing characteristics.

"This room is private," he said in a firm and angry tone, and vanished.

"That little..." began Rachel in a huff. "After all that

time I spent trying to find him, he just up and disappears. Oh, no he didn't'."She vanished as well, leaving Greg, Jackie, and I alone in Mr. Stilton's office and a lot of questions.

"We better go," I said.

Jackie and Greg both agreed. We cleaned up the taco wrappers, shoving them in the brown paper bag, and dumping them in the trash can on the sidewalk outside. Once we had gotten to Greg's car, my cell phone rang. It was Tiny and he sounded even worse than before.

"Mel," moaned Tiny, "I feel horrible."

I sympathized with him, but was unsure of what I could do about it. The only cure for a cold is to let it run its course.

"My nose is about to fall off. I swear it is. And I'm so stuffed up." He coughed into the receiver of his phone and I held mine away from my ear until he stopped.

"Where's Elise?" I asked.

"She's sick too," he cried.

I felt sorry for him. Never did I imagine that the day would come where I would see Tiny so helpless, but colds are like that. "I'll be right over."

I hung up and turned to Jackie and Greg. "You two go home without me."

Chapter 13

Greg had dropped me off at my car and I told him not to wait up for me; I had no idea how long I would be gone, but Tiny needed some help. I stopped at a Walgreen's, which was open 24 hours, and picked up some more supplies for severe colds, especially for nasal congestion, herbal tea for sore throats and colds, and a basketful of canned chicken noodle soup. The clerk gave me a weird look and stepped back a bit, no doubt worried that I was the one with the cold and she didn't want to catch it herself. I didn't blame her, but really, when you work in a public place, that is just something you have to deal with.

Once I had my bags of the standard cures for a cold, I drove over to Tiny's and let myself inside his apartment.

I found him where I had the last time I was here, on the couch with blankets wrapped around him like they were his own little cocoon.

"Tiny?"

Deep coughing greeted me. It appeared that he has moved beyond the sore throat stage to the congestion stage where all you do is cough and feel even more miserable than before. I felt his forehead. "You seem to be running a bit of a fever. Here."

I pulled out the thermometer I had also bought and stuck it under his tongue, after washing it with rubbing alcohol. 100 degrees. He had a slight fever all right. Though nothing unusual about that, some people do get a fever when they have a cold, I was a little concerned. I noticed a couple of empty beer bottles on the side table next to the couch and picked one up, waving it front of him with a disapproving look. "Really?"

"I don't like that herbal stuff," whined Tiny.

"That's it," I said. "I am making you some chicken soup and some tea and you will drink it."

Tiny moaned.

"I don't want any argument."

"I don't want to," said Tiny, sounding like a toddler who didn't want to take his nap.

"You will, or I will sic Rachel on you." I had no idea where she was at the time, but hoped that my threat would work.

Tiny's face contorted in a mixture of defiance and unease. He knew about Rachel, she had introduced herself to him when I had first met him, and her, almost two and half years ago. "You would too," he said.

Yes I would.

"Fine," Tiny huffed.

Now that we had gotten that out of the way, I went into his kitchen and pulled out a saucepan to heat the soup in and had decided to cook two cans, since I was also hungry. Jackie had eaten all of the tacos, leaving nothing for me or Greg. After I had the soup on the stove, I filled a kettle, which I had to clean first, with water and put it on a burner until it boiled.

"Here," I said to Tiny, carrying a tray with a cup of the herbal tea, glass of water, two nighttime capsules for relieving cold symptoms, and a bowl of soup.

He sat up and I placed the tray in his lap, watching as he brought the cup of tea up to his mouth and sipped it.

"Take your medicine too," I told him. I know I was treating him like a baby, but he was sort of acting like one, and someone had to make sure he got well, considering that Elise must have caught his cold and was stuck in her own bed.

Tiny popped the pills in his mouth and downed his glass of water.

"Now, I want you to eat all of your soup and drink all of your tea. And don't even think about giving it to the plant," I said, as I watched him from the corner of my eye try to pour the contents of his cup in the planter behind the couch. He stopped mid-pour and sat back down, disappointed that I had caught him, and drank his tea until it was gone.

The next hour was spent with me practically spoon-feeding Tiny his soup until I had gotten two bowlfuls in him, plus another cup of the herbal tea. Once done, I helped him into bed, pleased that the nighttime medicine had taken affect as he struggled to keep his eyes open.

After I had gotten him into bed, I ate the remainder of the soup, cleaned up, and left, but not before making certain that the next morning's breakfast had been prepared, which he could heat in the microwave once he woke up.

A giant yawn accompanied me as I got into my car and headed home. I checked the clock; it was no wonder I was so tired, since it was past midnight. That was it. It was time for bed.

Chapter 14

The next morning I woke up feeling a little tired and rundown. I forced myself out of bed. I couldn't afford to get sick or take a day off as I still needed to solve who broke into the stores on the shopping block, and why. Even though Mr. Stilton seemed to have closed the Candle Shoppe for the week, there were still my classes. I threw on my standby of jeans and a cami, with a sweater over it since one look out my window told me that it would be another cold, dreary, and snowy day. Would the snow ever stop?

A pile of stapled papers sat on my desk, reminding me that I had something important due today. That's right! A term paper for one of my classes was due and I found myself thankful that I had finished it last week, because with everything that has happened this week, there was no possible way I would have gotten it done.

My phone fell out of my pocket when I put on my coat, reminding me of last night's talk with the Candle Shoppe's resident ghost: Gregory King. It also made me think of Beverly. She wanted to speak with me about Roger, but Edmond interrupted her. Though he probably didn't mean to stop her from talking to us, but was just protective of his mother. Yet, Beverly did say that I could call her at any time. I fumbled in my pockets and found the slip of paper she had written her number on and dialed it. It went straight to voicemail.

"Beverly," I said, recording my message, "this is Mel. I wanted to know if we could meet up someplace today. I'd like to talk to you further about Roger."

I left my number and ended the call.

"Where are you going?" asked Jackie as I headed for the door.

I waved my paper in front her. She got that "Ah-ha" look on her face as she remembered my paper, and how I had spent all week last week stressing out about it.

"I need to drop this off, "I said, "and I think I will also stop by and see Detective Shorts."

"Okay. Bundle up, though. It looks nasty out there."

Nasty was putting it mildly. As I stepped outside into the parking lot, snow blasted me in the face, followed by a bitter cold wind that made me want to run back up to my apartment and curl up in a giant, fuzzy blanket. Knowing that I wouldn't be allowed to do such a thing,

I pulled my coat tighter around me and ran to my car, braving the snowstorm.

It took a little longer to get to the college than normal due to the weather and the fact that I drove slower than usual. At least I didn't have a class until later that day, but the one my paper was for wasn't meeting until next week and the teacher still wanted all of the papers by today.

I parked my car in a space near the building where all of the college professors had their offices and ran inside, hiking up the stairs two at a time. My professor wasn't in that day, which was little surprise, considering that he had mentioned something about taking a week off, but his office assistant was, and he was responsible for collecting the papers. I opened the door to the outer part of the office, not bothering to knock, breathless from having jogged up two flights of stairs.

"Another one?" said the office assistant.

"Yes," I replied and plopped the printed pages on the cluttered desk.

"You are the sixth person to hand one to me today," said the office assistant as he picked up my term paper and placed it in a folder where the others were kept. "I hope the rest of your classmates remember to bring theirs by. There are no exceptions for late papers."

"Not even when there's a snowstorm?" I said.

"Of course not. No exceptions is his policy."

I gave a weak smile, remembering how my professor had given an hour long speech one class period about how tardiness would not be tolerated. Thank goodness he was not here this week. I thanked the man and left just as my phone rang.

"Hello?" I answered, receiving a glare from someone passing by with an arm full of file folders, pointing at a sign that read, "No cell phones allowed."

Good grief. No one, not even the professors who had offices here, abided by such a policy.

"Mel," said the voice on the other end, "this is Beverly. You called me about wanting to meet."

"Yes, I need to talk to you more about what happened that night. I know that the weather is less than ideal, but I was hoping we could meet somewhere alone. For lunch, maybe?"

"I'm not afraid of a little snow," replied Beverly. "There is this little place, it's a diner of sorts…"

"Yes, I know it."

"I can be there in 20 minutes."

"I'll see you then."

I hurried to my car and drove over to the diner, taking great pains to keep my car from fishtailing every time I came to a red light. I had thought about calling Greg, or even Jackie, but decided against it. A one on one with Beverly might be better. I didn't want to intimidate her or scare her off and Rachel seemed to have been absent for now.

Beverly waved to me from a booth near a frosted window as I entered to diner. Grinning at her and waving back, I unzipped my coat and sat down, reveling in the aroma of sausage, eggs, and buttered waffles.

"It's a bit cold out there, isn't it?" said Beverly as I sat down.

"I think we're in for a bit of a storm," I replied, watching more snow come down heavier than before. My footprints on the sidewalk had already disappeared.

"May I take your order?" asked a waitress.

"I'll have your chicken and waffles and some coffee, please," I said.

"The same," said Beverly, not even bothering to glance at the menu.

The waitress wrote down our order, chewing on her wad of gum, and walked off, sticking her pencil behind her ear.

Just then, Rachel showed up, but remained invisible so that only I saw, or heard, her. "What's up?" she asked.

"Now, you had wanted to talk to me," said Beverly, unaware of Rachel's presence, something that I wanted to keep her unaware of.

"Yes," I said, while typing a message on the notepad feature of my phone for Rachel, asking her to follow Edmond. He seemed like a straightforward person, but I just wanted to be certain that he hadn't been putting on an act for our benefit, or Beverly's. "I have reason to believe that you might be right about Roger."

"How?" asked Beverly. "No one ever believed me."

"I'd rather not go into how I know." I positioned my phone so that Rachel could read the message, but Mrs. Waverly would not see it. "But I think there might have been someone else there that night who saw Brianna after he left her. I want you to tell me why you think he could never have done it."

"That's a great idea," said Rachel, referring to my

message, and disappeared, causing the napkins on the table to flip up and lay back down.

"Seems to be a bit of a breeze," muttered Beverly, watching the paper napkins.

"It's just, you are the only person to believe Roger's story," I said.

"I know Roger. He's like a second son to me. The man is very gentle and kindhearted. I just cannot image him doing what he is accused of doing to Brianna."

"Sometimes you don't know the people you care about," I said.

"I realize that, that can be true," replied Beverly, "but if you had ever seen them together, you would know that he could not have strangled her. Roger was devoted to Brianna."

"But people said that they saw them arguing that night."

"What was never publicized was the fact that Brianna was pregnant at the time. She had only just learned it herself and had come to me for guidance. You see, Roger was not the father."

"What?"

The waitress came back with our food and coffee and we remained silent until she had left.

"Before you judge, Brianna loved Roger. She said it happened one night when she went out with her friends and had a little too much to drink. She must have met a man there and one thing led to another. If she had been sober, it never would have happened.

"I had told her that she should tell Roger right away, but Brianna was afraid that he might leave her; so, she kept it a secret, but the night before the wedding, she couldn't do it anymore. She told Roger that night in the gazebo. Words were said and he left the party to clear his head.

"Roger told me later that even before he had learned of Brianna's death, he had decided to marry her anyway and raise the child as his own. He loved her that much and was willing to forgive her for her mistake."

"Are you sure he wasn't just saying that?"

"I know you have to ask, but if you had seen his face the day he learned of her death, you would have no doubt of his innocence. The man was torn apart and didn't speak to anyone for a week. The police and the D.A. took it as a sign of his guilt, but I knew better."

"Do you think that he could be the one breaking into those stores?" I asked.

"Roger is no thief," replied Beverly.

"He has been in prison for 20 years and that can change a person. You said that he always maintained his innocence. Isn't it possible that he believes those stores might have something that could prove it. It was a photography studio at the time of his incarceration and you said yourself that the man who owned it was hired to do the wedding pictures."

"It's possible. Poor Mr. King. He was a quirky individual, but I don't know much about him, other than that he loved photographing lightning. And we had one heck of a lightning storm that night. If only he hadn't gone out there when he did."

"Beverly," I said, recalling that she wanted to be called by her first name, "are you in contact with Roger?"

"What?"

"You are the only person who ever believed him and now he is back on the streets. I don't know about you, but if I were him, I would reach out to the one person who believed my innocence. Has he contacted you?"

"Yes," whispered Beverly.

"Will you tell me how I can reach him?"

Mrs. Waverly looked at me, unsure if she could trust me. I couldn't blame her. No one had ever believed her or Roger and I knew that she thought I might be setting a trap for him.

"Look, I know he has been breaking into the stores. It's the only thing that makes sense. No none else would have a reason to."

"He only searched the one store," said Beverly.

"Excuse me?" This was news.

"I searched the others."

"You do realize that that is a crime?" I said.

"I know." Beverly sighed in a manner that told me she was glad to get it all out. "I heard about the Candle Shoppe and knew it was Roger, so I met with him and warned him that if he got caught, he would go straight back to prison for the rest of his life. So, I volunteered to do the searching for him."

"What was he looking for?" I asked.

"It doesn't matter," Beverly replied. "I never found it. I'll talk to him and ask him to call you. You aren't going to turn him in, are you?"

"You admitted to committing a crime. I'm under obligation to tell the police."

"Please don't." Beverly's face looked worried and I pitied her. "Talk to Roger first. He will call you. I'll see to that. If you say anything now, he will be sent back to prison and we'll never learn who really killed Brianna."

I relented. I just couldn't tear out Mrs. Waverly's heart and I wanted to know who had murdered Beverly as well, if Roger was innocent. Besides, I still hadn't learned what he was looking for. "All right," I said. "I'll wait until after I talk to Roger, but I encourage you to tell the police about your involvement in the break-ins. You can't ask me to keep this a secret indefinitely."

"Fair enough. After you speak with Roger, I'll tell the police myself."

We finished our meal and paid our check, with Beverly promising me, again, that she would turn herself in to the police after I had met with Roger.

Once we parted, I ran into none other than Jillian. If I never saw that woman again, it wouldn't be soon enough.

"Stirring up the past, are we?" she asked in a snide tone.

"There is no 'we'," I growled at her.

"So, how does it feel, no longer having the trust of the public behind you?"

"Why don't you tell me?" I spat.

"Miss Summers!" Up walked Detective Henderson. "I was hoping that I would run into you." She looked at Jillian. "Is there something you need?"

"I was just talking with Mel, here," replied Jillian.

"Your conversation will have to wait," said Detective Henderson. "I don't think you know…"

"I know who you are, Miss Modsen," snapped Detective Henderson. "But if you'll excuse me, I have some important matters to discuss with Miss Summers."

Detective Henderson held her arm out, indicating that I should follow her, which I was more than happy to do just to get away from Jillian, and led me down the walk with a disappointed Jillian skulking away.

"I happened to be passing by," said Detective Henderson, "and I noticed you speaking to Mrs. Waverly."

"Happened?" I replied. "You mean you were following me."

"I wouldn't…"

"Cut to the chase, detective," I said. I did not appreciate being followed and I knew that this was no chance meeting.

"As you wish. You remember that I had wanted you to find a way to speak with her. Well, now you have and I am most interested in what she told you."

"You might also recall that I never agreed to help you. I had run into her by chance yesterday and she invited me out for lunch today."

"Must I remind you that if she said anything that pertains to this case, you are obligated to tell me."

"I am under no such obligation." I did my best to keep a straight face. I had promised Beverly that I would say nothing about the break-ins, at least for a few days, giving her the chance to come forward on her own. I wasn't about to go back on my word. "She reiterated her belief of Roger Croukman's innocence."

That much was true enough.

Detective Henderson gave me a doubtful look, but I had no intention of telling her what she wanted to know. "Detective Shorts always spoke highly of you."

"He also never asked me to do his job for him."

"No… you just tend to do it anyway."

She started to get on my nerves. I didn't know this woman. What did she think I was? Someone to just help her out because she wanted me to? "Will that be all, detective?"

"For now. And, might I remind you, impeding a police investigation is a crime."

"So everyone keeps telling me, but if you all knew how to do your jobs in the first place, you wouldn't need me to do it for you."

I could have kicked myself for saying that last part. Me and my pride; one of these days it would get me into trouble. Before Detective Henderson could say anything, or do anything, I left and hurried down the icy sidewalk.

"OOOO," said Rachel when I had gotten a few yards away. "Look at you, getting an attitude with the cops. I may make a spunky woman out of you yet."

I looked at her, wondering how long she had been there and realized that she had probably overheard the entire exchange between me and the detective. "Anything interesting about Edmond?" I asked, changing the subject.

"The guy is a complete bore," said Rachel. "He didn't do much. Picked up a few groceries for his mother and ran a few other errands. Honestly, he didn't do anything out of the ordinary. You might be wrong about him on this one."

It was possible. Edmond had been helpful and courteous. "What about the groundskeeper?"

"Donald? Not much either. He's shifty and doesn't seem to trust anyone, not to mention his personality lacks a bit of friendliness. but I didn't notice anything that screamed murderer."

"Thanks, Rachel." I still didn't like Mrs. Waverly's

groundskeeper. Something about him seemed familiar and I couldn't shake the feeling that I had seen him before. "Keep me informed will you?"

"Sure thing!" She vanished, leaving me alone on the sidewalk among the swirling snow that dropped from the sky, forming a thick blanket on the ground. If it didn't let up, we would be buried under millions of ice crystals.

My phone buzzed. Jackie had sent me a text with a link in it. I tapped on the link and suddenly wished I hadn't. Jillian had posted another article about me that morning, which explained why I ran into her a few minutes ago; she wanted more dirt on me.

A Psychic Indeed

Jillian Modsen

Self-proclaimed psychic, Mellow Summers, shows no inclination that she knows anything about the latest string of break-ins, nor has she been able to lead police to the person responsible for an attempt on the life of a local police detective.

In looking into Miss Summers' previous encounters with the police, it becomes clear that she suffers from delusions of grandeur. Her friends fair little better, accompanying her on her amateur sleuthing as she rushes to investigate what should be left to the local police, thus endangering herself and the lives of others.

One example of the blundering of this supposed psychic is the Pen Mills Estate, a landmark in these parts, that no longer exists. Though she did assist in capturing a band of thieves, and recovering the Rose pendant, Miss Summers' rash actions resulted in the burning down of this historic landmark. It didn't have to happen that way. After learning where the thieves were, all she had to do was call the police and let them do their jobs. After all, as a psychic, she must have known that her actions would lead to the destruction of a structure that was worth more than all of the cases she has supposedly helped solve combined.

Perhaps our overly enthusiastic psychic ought to take a vacation before we lose another treasured piece of history.

And let us not forget that Miss Summers, herself, was once the prime suspect in a murder investigation. Her only defense at the time was that she remembered nothing. That doesn't bode well if you are supposed to have mediumistic abilities. The charges were eventually dropped by the District Attorney, who took a month long vacation afterwards, though it is unclear why.

That bitch. Words could not convey what I thought or felt about her. Didn't her editor see that she was on some sort of crusade to destroy me? Or were these articles bringing in new readership that he didn't care, so long as the number of subscriptions to the local paper went up.

I didn't know if there as anything I could do about this. Jillian wasn't wrong about the Pen Mills Estate. After I had helped Rachel solve her murder, I ran into another ghost that had insisted that he had been murdered there. As it turned out, he had died from a severe asthma attack, but there had had been a string of robberies around town at the same time and the people involved had taken up residence at the estate. It had been abandoned and most locals feared going there because of stories about it being haunted, stories that turned out to be true. I did find the thieves there and Jackie and I were tied up and left to die, after our captors had set the place on fire to cover their tracks.

I guess one could argue that it was sort of my fault that the Pen Mills Estate had burned down, being reduced to smoldering ruins that the city had still done nothing with. Though, Greg had once told me that they probably would have set the place on fire anyway, but such a statement did little to comfort me. I still felt bad about it.

And the bit about me being a prime suspect in a murder investigation wasn't too far off either. Soon after the Pen Mills fiasco, I had woken up in a strange motel room covered in someone else's blood. Later, a corpse showed up and the D.A. pointed his finger at me. If it hadn't been for Rachel and my aunt Ethel, I don't think I ever would have proven my innocence.

I stood on the sidewalk, wondering what I should do. I didn't feel like going home and I had a class later in the afternoon. In the end, I decided to go visit Detective Shorts. He must have been going stir crazy in the hospital.

As it turned out, the detective wasn't going as crazy as I thought. I found him sitting up in his bed, reading through police reports, looking rather spry for someone who had gotten shot two days ago.

"Miss Summers," he said. "What a surprise."

"I thought I would check in on you," I replied. "See how you were doing."

"Well enough. These doctors still won't let me go though."

I smiled a bit. "It shouldn't be too much longer."

"So, I hear that you have been enlisted to help the new Detective Henderson."

"Not really."

"What did she ask you to do?"

"She wanted me to speak with Beverly Waverly."

Detective Shorts' eyebrows arched. "So she is looking into that possible connection."

"What can you tell me about her?"

"Probably nothing that you haven't already been able to figure out. And I don't want you looking into it."

Too late. And he should know by now that I never back away from something like this.

"You should also know that I am starting to believe that she was right about Roger."

What? That was news. "What do you mean?"

"As I said before, when the flower shop was broken into, I decided to start looking into the old case files. I knew that the strip had been a photography studio once. The owner of that studio was the photographer for Roger

Croukman's wedding. I thought it strange that soon after he is released from prison these break-ins took place."

"And that is what made you change your mind?"

"There were discrepancies in the way the investigation was conducted, but what made me change my mind was the fact that someone took a shot at me. The only person who would do that would be the real murderer. Roger would have no reason to get rid of a detective trying to prove his innocence, besides the fact that he has a solid alibi."

"How do you know that it wasn't someone you've angered in the past by arresting them?" I asked.

"It's a possibility, but the timing tells me that it is more than mere coincidence."

I checked my watch. It was almost time for my class. "I'll see you later."

"I mean it, Mel," said Detective Shorts, using my nickname, something he never did unless he was worried about me getting into trouble, "be careful. If you keep probing into this, you might become the next target."

"I'll be fine."

"I could give Tiny a call. I'm sure he would keep you out of trouble."

"Tiny is out of commission due to a severe cold. I was at his place yesterday, forcing him to take some medicine."

"I would have loved to have seen that," chuckled Detective Shorts and I knew he was picturing me force-feeding Tiny cough syrup.

"Anyway, I do have a class to get to."

Detective Shorts gave me a look, the one that says he knew I was up to something, but chose to remain quiet.

Chapter 15

When I arrived at the college, it looked as though it had been buried under snow, almost like mother nature was trying to wipe its memory from existence. I parked as close to the building where my class was located as I could, but everyone else had the same idea. The wind ripped the car door from my hands, blasting me with shards of pin-sized ice as I got out and bolted to the double doors, relieved when I walked through them and into the warmth that awaited me inside.

The faces of students stared at me. Great. They must have read Jillian's latest about me. I ignored them and hurried down the hall, my sneakers squeaking against the floor with each step.

"Hey, look," said one student, munching on an ice

cream sandwich, "it's our psychic! How long is this storm going to last?"

Before he knew it, something ripped his ice cream sandwich from his hands and smacked him in the face with it, smearing vanilla ice cream all over. "Why don't you shut up?" said Rachel, remaining invisible.

I continued to my class and sat in the first available seat.

"I can't stand these idiots." Rachel appeared in the desk next to me. "Predict this. Predict that. As though that is how all of this works."

"Rachel," I whispered as her voice attracted some odd looks.

"What?"

"You're attracting attention."

"Good!"

Someone walked in with his arms full of books and papers, fumbling with them as he navigated his way to an empty desk. Rachel watched and I knew she planned something because she got that mischievous look on her face.

"What out! It bites!" she screamed at the poor man, causing him to jump. She ignored my disapproving glare as she cackled with glee, pleased with herself.

She spotted a piece of paper hanging on the blackboard with my picture on it: one of Jillian's stories about me. I had noticed it when I came in, but chose to ignore it, thinking that if I didn't bring attention to it, maybe this whole thing would blow over. Rachel, on the other hand, was a different story. She snatched the paper from its position on the board and held it up in midair, frightening the people in the classroom.

"Who did this?" she demanded, waving the yellowed

paper amidst a bunch of wide-eyed people who couldn't understand what was happening. She must have realized that they didn't see her because she materialized in front of them. "Who!" She stamped her foot.

No one said anything. No doubt they were having trouble comprehending the fact that a ghost screamed at them.

"May-may-maybe the last class did it," stammered one person in the front of the class.

Rachel glared at him, her hand on her hip as she held the paper article about me.

"So you all think this is funny."

"No," said the same person.

"What am I supposed to do about this?" demanded Rachel, ignoring the faces that gawked at her, though I think a part of her was having a little too much fun with this.

"Maybe you should make the author eat it," said another person in the room.

Oh no. I buried my face in my hands. I knew what was going to happen next. Rachel's eyes gleamed and a devilish look crossed her face and she vanished, with the paper.

Long exhales filled the room from those who had held their breaths, still shocked that an angry ghost chewed them out.

Rachel popped back in the room. "By the way, class is dismissed!" She vanished again.

Everyone left. I couldn't blame them and a part of me was thankful for it, since I did not want to be there myself. Before the professor arrived, I hurried out of the room. My mind wandered to the photographer and his riddles. Could he have seen something he wasn't supposed to?

What I needed was an actual blue print of the photography studio before it got converted. I dialed Jack and he answered on the first ring.

"Jack?"

"Not again," he groaned.

"Jack, I need your help."

"You always need my help."

"Do you know if the original building of the photography studio was ever torn down."

"Actually, I do, and I don't need to look that up. It used to take up that whole block. When the owner died and the bank resold the property to a developer, instead of tearing it down, the guy decided to remodel the building into four distinct stores, which he leases. The original structure is still there, but the modifications make it difficult to see that."

That was good to know. "Is there any way you can get me the blueprints of the original studio?"

"Why?"

"Can you?"

"I can, but the real question is: will I."

"Jack."

"Okay. Okay. I will. Give me some time to find them and I'll send them to you."

"Thanks."

I headed to the local library, deciding that I needed to look up some old articles concerning the events from 20 years ago. When I entered, I saw the paper with my picture on the front page sitting on the front desk. Angered by it, and fed up with Jillian's attempts to discredit me, I snatched it, crumbled it up, and tossed it in the nearby trash can.

The archives were in the basement, so I took the stairs down to it. I never liked elevators much and the exercise wouldn't hurt me.

"Excuse me?" I said to the plump lady at the desk when I entered the archives room. "I need some help in locating old newspaper articles."

"What year?" asked the woman in a bored tone, looking over the rims of her reading glasses at me. "Oh, it's you."

I gaped at her. I had never met her before in my life. How could she… The articles by Jillian. It seems, whether I wanted it or not, my face had become as recognizable in this town as the face of any celebrity.

"All archived newspapers are over there. Some are bound into books. Others are on microfiche."

Realizing that I would never get any help from her, I moseyed over to the area where she indicated the old newspapers were. First, I looked through the bound books, having never been a fan of microfiche, as the fast scrolling film tends to make me seasick. Most of the articles revealed nothing that I didn't already know, but one caught my eye.

A picture of Edmond Waverly stared back at me from the stained page and he looked irate. I skimmed the article.

Despite their lifelong friendship, Edmond Waverly testified against Roger Croukman during the trial. Though the details have not been released to the press, it is believed that Edmond Waverly, a wall street broker who lives in New York City and had returned for his friend's wedding, gave pertinent information that will seal Mr. Croukman's conviction for the murder of his fiancé Brianna Grafton.

Read *Mother Mourns* on page 9A for more.

Testified against Roger? Why is it Beverly kept that a secret? I could understand why Edmond said nothing, but keeping something like this buried made me wonder about the both of them. Was Beverly covering for her son?

I flipped through the book, looking for page 9A, but it wasn't there. Instead, all I found was a written note that read, "Microfiche 368925." Great. Guess I was going to have to sit in front of that behemoth of a machine anyway.

I yanked open the drawer, receiving a glare from the lady at the desk. What did she think I was going to do? Run off with it? My fingers zipped through the plastic cases that held the film until I found the one I searched for.

"Excuse me?" I said to the woman at the desk. "Can I get some help with this?" I pointed at the machine.

The woman ignored me and swiveled around in her chair, turning her back on me.

Okay. Fine. I'll do it myself. It took me a few minutes, but I figured out how to thread the film into the humming machine, sweating from the heat that was released from it, forming a sweltering hothouse.

"SHHH!" the lady shouted at me as I zipped through the film, my stomach doing loopy-loops from the scrolling images and text, until I found page 9A. Geez, lady, give it a rest. An image of Beverly crying against her son's shoulder filled the screen.

> Heartbreak has riddled the Waverly household as the trial continues in the Roger Croukman case. Mrs. Waverly has refused to comment on her son's testimony, insisting that Mr. Croukman is innocent. A verdict is expected tomorrow.

The rest of the article was blurred and faded, making it impossible to read, but I had learned some of what I needed to know. Edmond and Beverly had both neglected to tell me about his testimony against Roger Croukman, and I intended to find out why.

My phone buzzed as I received a text from Jackie. *Where are you?*

I sent a reply. *At the library. On my way home.*

I put the film away, back where I had gotten it from and made certain that the books were placed back on the shelf in their proper order, all under the watchful gaze of the library attendant.

"You're going to burn in hell," said the lady as I walked passed.

I clamped my mouth shut to keep from uttering a retort. It wouldn't have done any good and I needed to get back home. There wasn't much else I could do at the library.

Rachel showed up, holding out the crumpled newspaper she had taken from the classroom I had been in earlier that day. "Okay, so I was unable to find that reporter so that I could make her eat this."

I didn't say anything.

"What?"

I pointed at the library attendant. Horror filled her face as her mouth hung open, exposing her bridgework.

"BOO!" Rachel yelled at her, causing the woman to tip backward in her chair and crash into the floor.

I tried to help the woman up, amidst Rachel's hysterical cackles of laughter, but she slapped my hand away.

"Get away!" yelled the woman.

I pulled away and left, followed by a floating piece of paper that vanished into thin air once I got outside.

When I pulled into the parking lot of my apartment complex, the giant flakes of falling snow formed a veil, making it impossible to see anything, including my hand when I put it directly in front of my face. At first, I had planned on going to the Candle Shoppe to see if there was something I could do to help out, but Jackie had texted me while I drove home, informing me that Mr. Stilton had decided to close up for the next several days. That was fine by me. I had no desire to go out in this mess and curling up in front of the television to watch *The Walking Dead* on Netflix, while drinking hot chocolate, was a more attractive idea.

I had no idea where Rachel had gone to and hadn't seen her since the incident at the library. She always did her own thing and my money was on the fact that she busied herself with harassing Jillian Modsen. If Jillian didn't believe in ghosts now, she either would be a believer by the time Rachel got through with her, or at least have a very bad week and maybe give up this crusade to discredit me.

"Miss Summers?" A soft voice stopped me before I could enter the building.

I turned around and found a man—his tattered and stained coat looked as though it was never meant to keep anyone warm in weather like this—standing in the shadows, doing his best not to be seen by anyone, except me.

"May I help you?" I asked, gripping the door handle and ready to run inside should he try anything.

"Beverly... Beverly Waverly said you wished to speak with me," said the man, his white-streaked beard jiggled with each move he made, though it looked as though it could still use a comb. "I'm Roger Croukman."

I released me grip on the door handle. That was fast. I know that Mrs. Waverly had said that she would ask him to come see me, but I hadn't expected it to be this quick.

"Won't you come in?" I asked him.

"I'd rather stay out here, if you don't mind."

I moved away from the door and further into the shadows, behind a concrete column so that we could have some privacy.

"I understand that you are looking into the break-ins."

"Well, the place where I work was one of the stores that had been targeted. Beverly already told me that she had done the other three."

"You can't blame her," Roger said. "She was just trying to help me and keep me from getting into any more trouble."

"But you were the one that had broken into the Candle Shoppe."

"Yes."

"I told Beverly that she is going to have to turn herself in for that, otherwise I'll have to. And you need to too."

"If I do that, then I will go back to prison and may never be allowed out."

"You knew that even when you broke into the Candle Shoppe."

Roger looked at his feet in shame.

"Why don't you tell me why you broke in in the first place. Nothing was taken, so you must have been search-ing for something in particular."

Roger wrung his hands; his jittery nature made me wish that I had been more gentle with my words instead of lecturing him.

"Does this have to do with Brianna's murder?" I asked, hoping I wouldn't scare him off.

"Yes," he whispered. "Brianna had asked me to meet with her in the gazebo. I thought that she wanted some time alone, but instead, she wanted to tell me about her pregnancy. I was angry at first and went for a long walk while I tried to grapple with everything and figure things out. I didn't do it. I know that everyone says I did, but I never…"

"I believe you," I said.

"Gregory was more than just a photographer," said

Roger. "He was my friend. Oh, I wish he hadn't gone out in that storm that night. If he hadn't, he'd still be here. And I'm not saying that just because I believe he could prove my innocence. He was a good man."

"So why the break-ins?" I prompted, trying to get back on tract.

"Gregory had his oddities. As a photographer, he would take far more photographs than would ever be developed or bought by the people who hired him. On a normal gig, he could use as much as 20 rolls of film, but only 10 would ever get developed. It might seem wasteful, but that was how he was. This was more a hobby than a job.

"He also had this habit of grabbing three or four rolls of film that had been used on any given job and hiding them somewhere. He said that doing so was good luck."

"So, what does this have to do with the night of Brianna's murder?" I asked, trying to follow where Roger went.

"During the party, Gregory had set up over 30 cameras to take snapshots at certain intervals. These intermittent shots were meant to capture the essence of the party without having people pose. Candid photography, as he called it. He still took a few posed photographs, but he liked the unrehearsed stuff as well. There was a camera set up just outside the gazebo. If it's timer worked, it would have been taking photographs throughout the night and it might have captured a shot of the real murderer.

"When the party had ended, and before anyone had discovered Brianna"—Roger's voice cracked when he said her name and I handed him a tissue from my purse—"Gregory would have taken the film out of the cameras and placed them in their cases. If I know him, he would have gone back to his studio and picked a few rolls at random to stash away for posterity. What if one of those rolls is from the camera at the gazebo?"

That was a possibility and a question worth answering, but a part of me doubted that such a thing could be possible. "That is a big if," I said, "and we are talking about 20 years here and a building that had been modified and turned into four separate stores."

"It is worth looking for," said Roger. "I have already lost 20 years of my life."

"All right," I said. It was worth looking for it and what did I have to lose? "I will help you, but on one condition: you meet me at the Candle Shoppe at midnight tonight. No more breaking in on your own. And Beverly stays home."

"Agreed."

"You do realize, though, that this is a longshot, and if we don't find anything, you are going to have to let it go."

Roger hung his head, not liking the idea, but knew I was right. "Fine."

As I looked at his disheartened face, I thought about what I had learned at the library that day. "Roger, do you know why Edmond testified against you at the trial?"

"He was in love with Brianna."

What? That was another piece of information Edmond had left out. Again, a part of me could understand why. Such emotions and memories are painful and perhaps he did not want to think about it. "Did Beverly know?"

"No. He did a good job of hiding it. He was even the first to congratulate me when Brianna and I announced our engagement. Despite his initial feelings for her, he seemed okay with us getting married. But when Brianna died, I guess he believed what the papers and the police had said. I lost everything that night."

"I'm sorry," I said, patting his frozen, bare hand. The poor man didn't even have a pair of gloves, so I gave him mine.

"What…"

"For your hands," I said. "They've got to be cold."

"I can't…"

"Take them," I insisted, shoving my gloves into his calloused and blistered hands. "Fashion is overrated and I can always buy new ones."

Roger took them and put them on, thankful that someone cared enough to give him something to keep his hands warm.

"Midnight," I said.

He nodded his head and walked off while I went inside and walked up the stairwell to my floor.

"Hey, I was wondering when you were going to get back," said Jackie as I walked through the door to the apartment. "This snow is really coming down."

"No kidding."

"Greg's home. He said he got a call telling him not to bother coming in. Closed due to bad weather."

"Good, because we're going to need him."

Jackie put down what she had been fiddling with and came closer. "Need him?"

"I ran into Roger Croukman just a few minutes ago," I said.

Jackie's eyes widened and her jaw dropped. "What?"

"Mrs. Waverly had asked him to see me and he met me down in the parking lot as I got out of my car. He and Beverly were the ones committing the break-ins. They were looking for some rolls of film. I told him that I would meet him at midnight at the Candle Shoppe and I was hoping you and Greg would come along."

"Really? How will we know where to start looking?" asked Jackie.

"We'll need to talk to the photographer's ghost again." My phone buzzed and a text message with images of the original blueprints to the studio popped up on the small screen. "And I have the original blueprints. I had Jack look them up."

"Well, of course I'm coming."

A knock sounded at the door. Thinking it might be Greg coming over, I ripped it open. "Greg, I… oh."

Father Hillard stood in the doorway and he must have noticed the disappointed tone in my voice when I saw him. "I know that I'm not much to look at, nor was I expected, but I'm sure you can do a better greeting than 'oh'."

"Sorry, I thought you were someone else."

"I gathered that."

I noticed an overnight bag in his hands. "What's that?"

"Detective Shorts called me, expressing his concern that you might do something which would put your life in danger. So, he asked me to keep an eye on you."

"I am perfectly capable…" I began.

"It's not up for negotiation," said Father Hillard. "I will sleep on the floor if necessary, but the detective was insistent."

Of course he was. Detective Shorts must have known I was planning something the moment I left his hospital room. Knowing I would never get out of this, I let Father Hillard inside and pointed at the couch. I couldn't tell Greg my plans now. How was I going to sneak out with Father Hillard guarding the front door? I couldn't climb out the window. It was too high up.

Father Hillard set his overnight bag down and noticed the TV, which I had turned on the moment I had gotten home. "What were you girls planning to watch?"

"*The Walking Dead,*" I answered and his face conveyed disapproval.

"Not one of my favorite shows."

"Not one of your favorites!" Jackie blurted out. "How can you not like it? And Daryl—what a hottie! I love his toned muscles and the facial hair and…" Jackie continued her retinue of why she loved Daryl's character so much before she noticed Father Hillard's questioning look.

"Not that you would care about such things," said Jackie in an effort to reclaim her dignity. I swear that if she could marry the actor, she would.

"Popcorn, anyone?" asked Jackie, her face turning red from embarrassment.

"Put it on whatever you want," I said to Father Hillard before going into the kitchen to help Jackie.

"Now what are we going to do?" whispered Jackie to me.

"I don't know," I said, rubbing my throat as it had started to feel scratchy.

Having him here put a crimp in my plans. I didn't know how we were going to get away without him knowing about it.

Jackie put popcorn into the popcorn maker and we waited until it started popping before discussing our plans further.

"Maybe he'll go to sleep early," said Jackie. "He's old. Old people don't stay up very late."

"It's a possibility," I said. "I told Roger that I would be there by midnight. Why don't we pretend to go to bed at nine. He should be asleep by then."

"One can only hope." Jackie popped her head out the kitchen doorway and watched as Father Hillard continued to surf channels. "You text Greg and tell him our plans. We'll sneak out at 11 and meet him down there by 11:30."

"Deal." I pulled out my phone and sent a text to Greg. *Urgent. Need to meet you at the Candle Shoppe by 11:30 tonight. Explain later.*

He responded, *OK.*

"Greg says he'll meet us," I told Jackie, keeping my voice low so that Father Hillard wouldn't hear me. I felt a little bad about making these secretive plans when he had promised Detective Shorts that he would keep an eye on us, but I couldn't ask him to come along.

"So how are we to get out? He's sleeping on the couch."

"We'll pretend to go to bed at around nine and wait for him to fall asleep," I said. "Once he has, we'll sneak out. Once we're out the door, he can't stop us."

"Okay."

My plan sounded simple enough and I couldn't think

of any other way. Besides, he was old, well older, so how late could he stay up anyway? We hurried up with the popcorn and walked into the living room as though everything was normal. He had settled on watching *Casablanca* and we sat next to him, with the popcorn in the middle and individual bowls for serving. I spent most of the time watching the clock and counting down the minutes until nine.

Chapter 16

"Ow!" hissed Jackie, tripping over a small bag that had not yet made it to the storage area as we tiptoed down the hallway to the door of our apartment.

I shushed her and pointed at the lump on the couch that was Father Hillard. He hadn't moved. I took two steps into the living room and leaned over, checking the mound on the couch wrapped under a pile of blankets. A soft snore emanated from them and I breathed a sigh of relief. He was still sleeping.

My flashlight fell from my purse, thanks to me forgetting to zip it all the way closed. In a mad dash, I reached for it, fumbling with it as it evaded my grasp and caught it just before it struck the floor. Balancing on one foot, while holding my flashlight, I glanced at Jackie who watched me with a worried expression, cringing from the possibility of my waking up our guest. I placed my other foot on the floor and stuffed the flashlight in my bag, zipping it shut and motioned for Jackie to come forward and we both crept to the door, grabbing our keys. I opened the door, afraid that the hallway's light might wake Father Hillard, but he never moved from his position on the couch. We slipped into the corridor and I shut the door.

"Glad that's over," said Jackie. "I thought for sure that he was going to wake up."

"Yeah, well, let's go before he notices we're gone," I said.

"It's a little late for that."

We froze. Both Jackie and I turned around to find Father Hillard standing behind us with his coat and boots on.

"How did…" began Jackie.

"You two are not as quiet as you might think," said Father Hillard. "And though I am older; I am not that old."

Jackie and I looked at our feet in shame.

"I overheard you talking this afternoon."

"But the blankets on the couch," said Jackie.

"You are not the first generation to invent sneaking out of the house. Stuffed pillows underneath the blankets may be an old trick, but it works every time. And the snore app on my smartphone proved quite useful."

"Snore app?" I asked.

"Yes," said Father Hillard, "I was surprised to find one, but it worked."

"I guess they do have an app for everything," commented Jackie.

"Look, I'm not going back in," I said. "I need to get down to the Candle Shoppe and I promised to meet someone down there."

"I'm not going to make you stay," said Father Hillard, "but I am coming with you."

I started to protest, but he interrupted me.

"It's not open for negotiation."

Knowing I would never get out of taking him with us, I agreed to his demands and headed to the stairwell that led to the parking lot.

We piled into his car, which had been built to handle snowy conditions, and drove down to the Candle Shoppe. Greg was already there, waiting for us. He gave me a questioning look when he saw Father Hillard, but I shook my head in a "don't ask" gesture. The only other person we needed was Roger. I saw no sign of him and started to think that he had chosen not to come when he saw Greg and Father Hillard, but my fears were soon put to rest when he walked up.

"Miss Summers," he said, his voice low, "who are..."

"They're friends," I said. "They're here to help us search for the film."

Of course, the one person I really needed was Rachel, but she was nowhere to be found. I led everyone to the door of the Candle Shoppe and opened it with the key that I still had. Once inside, I closed the door and turned on a lamp, while pulling out my phone that had the blueprints Jack had sent me.

"Now what?" asked Greg.

"Well, according to these blueprints, that wall was not originally here, but that one was."

"You mind explaining what we are looking for?" asked Father Hillard and I was reminded that he had no idea who Roger was, or why we were at the Candle Shoppe in the first place.

I faced him, unsure of how I was going to tell him who Roger was and what I had planned. "Um... this is Roger Croukman. He was..."

"Yes, I know who he is," said Father Hillard.

"He says that there is proof of his innocence locked away here and we had decided to help him search for it."

"That was a long time ago," said Father Hillard. "The odds..."

"I know what the odds are," said Roger, his voice firm.

"Very well, I will help you as it seems to be the only way to keep an eye on you."

I checked the blueprints on my phone and had Greg help me look at the wall that matched one of the original structures. As much as I hated doing it, I picked up something heavy and used it to rip a hole open in the wall.

"Mel!" yelled Jackie, surprised by my antics.

"Mr. Stilton can take the repairs out of my paycheck, but I need to know what is in there."

Greg helped me pull the drywall away and shined a flashlight in there, but we found no cubbies or anything that could have been used to hide a few rolls of film. What I really needed was Rachel and the photographer's ghost.

"Wish Rachel were here," I whispered to Greg.

Sometimes I wonder if Rachel is around me all of the time, but chooses to remain unseen, because at that moment, she burst in, saying, "Your wish is my command!"

Father Hillard dropped his flashlight and took two steps back in surprise after watching Rachel materialize in full form with her arms raised. Taking one look at his shocked face, Rachel faded and leaned in close to whisper in my ear. "That guy is staring at me."

"Probably because he has never really seen a ghost. And I am pretty certain this is the first time one just showed up right in front of him."

"Oh." She made herself look more solid and approached the priest. "Hi. I'm Rachel. Mel's ethereal other half when it comes to solving crime."

Father Hillard just stared at her, unsure of what to do.

"You know, you're supposed…" Rachel began to lecture him, but I cut her off.

"Rachel! We need to speak to Gregory, the photographer that used to work here."

"Yeah, he's been a bit difficult to track down., but I'll get him. Give me a sec."

"So, that is Rachel?" asked Father Hillard, forcing his voice to remain calm.

"You've heard of her?" asked Jackie.

"Detective Shorts had mentioned her from time to time, but I never fully believed him when he said she was…"

"Dead?" said Jackie.

At that moment, Rachel popped in, holding Gregory by the shoulders, dragging him into the room. He flailed his arms against her and almost got free of her grasp, but Rachel seized him by his belt and yanked him forward.

"Now you listen to me," she said through gritted

teeth, "you're coming in here. No more riddles. No more nonsense. Get you ghostly little behind…"

The photographer broke free of her grasp and vanished. "What? That little…" Rachel disappeared as well, leaving us all standing there with dumbfounded looks on our faces.

They reappeared, locked in a struggle with Rachel trying to pin him down and force him to stay put. "Now, I'm tired of your nonsense!" she yelled at Gregory.

He vanished again.

"Don't worry," said Rachel, flipping a strand of hair out of her face. "I'll get him." She vanished.

"What is this?" asked Greg. "*WWF Raw* ghost style?"

I shrugged my shoulders. Like the others, I just stood there and watched as Rachel struggled with the photographer in an effort to get him to talk to us.

They reappeared. Gregory tried to make a break for it, but Rachel must have been ready because she seized him and threw whim against the wall and pinned him down. Not that I can explain how one ghost is able to pin another ghost against a solid wall, but I wasn't about to ask. I had other things on my mind.

"Don't you move again," huffed Rachel, "or I swear I will kick you ethereal butt from here to eternity!"

Gregory stopped and looked at all of us. I glanced at Roger. If he was scared, he never showed it. Perhaps he was so desperate to prove his innocence that he didn't care if he saw a real ghost. Though, I'm sure he had seen those articles about me by Jillian and perhaps he sought me out because of it, besides Beverly's insistence.

I glanced over at Father Hillard, who still had a shocked expression on his face, but managed to remain calm; well, calm enough so that he didn't run from the building screaming bloody murder.

"Gregory," I said, "I need to know if you remember the night Brianna was murdered?"

"Memories are fickle and can often lead one into a pickle," replied Gregory.

"Oh, for crying out loud," said an exasperated Rachel, "will you give her a straight answer?"

"Please," I tried again, "do you remember that night?"

"I remember thunder and lightning on the prowl," said Gregory, "a perfect night for murder most fowl."

"I am going to kill him," said Rachel.

"He's already…" began Greg, but one look from Rachel's murderous face stopped him.

"Gregory…" I began again, but Roger stepped forward and interrupted me."

"Gregory, do you know me?" He allowed the thin light from the lamp to fall on his aged face as he stared into Gregory's ghostly eyes. "It's me, Roger."

Gregory's eyes lit up and he took on a more solid form. I'm not sure what happened, but something much have clicked, bringing him into our reality and away from his own. "Roger? You've aged."

"20 years," said Roger, his voice becoming more calm.

"20… has it been that long?"

"Yes," said Roger.

The rest of us just watched, though Rachel crossed her arms and pursed her lips.

"Brianna…I'm sorry. I should never have gone out that night, but you know how much I loved photographing lightning."

"I know."

"I don't remember it. I guess a part of me knew, but I didn't want to believe it and came back here anyway. It's the only place that ever felt like home."

"Gregory," said Roger, "I need to know. Did you bring home the rolls of film?"

"Yes, yes, I always emptied the cameras and packed everything up. All of the film was deposited in the development room, except for three."

"What do you mean?" I asked, but wished I hadn't because that seemed to have broken whatever hold on reality Gregory had.

"Three is a most powerful number, and so three were left asunder."

"He's fading again," muttered Jackie.

"Gregory, please," said Roger. "I need to know what you did with the film."

"In a wall among flowers," said Gregory and I knew he had reverted back to his riddles, "there it stays hour upon hour."

"Gregory," Roger pressed again, "where is the development room."

"Dark and deep below, is all you need know."

Gregory vanished once again, leaving us all alone to wade through his nonsensical information.

"Why that little…" began Rachel, gearing up to go after him again.

"Rachel," I said, stopping her. "I don't think going after him is going to solve anything."

"But, Mel," said Jackie, "we were so close."

"I know," I said, feeling horrible because it was my pushiness that made him leave.

"Let's look at those blueprints," said Greg. "Every photo studio has a darkroom for film development. Maybe they will tell us where it was."

"A cellar," said Father Hillard.

"What?" said Greg.

We all turned and face the priest.

"You all are not very good with riddles, are you?" said Father Hillard. "'Deep below' means underground. All cellars or basements are underground."

"But there is no record of one having every been here," I said, looking at the blueprints on my phone.

"That doesn't mean that it isn't there," said Father Hillard. "I've lived here a long time and before this place was even a photo studio it was a winery."

"A what?"

"Did a lot of remodeling, which mostly consisted of tearing down all of the old structures and building a new one: the studio. There could still be a cellar that might have been sealed off when the studio was erected. Of course, since it was always here, it would never have been included in the original blueprints of the photography studio."

"So how do we find it?" I asked.

"Leave that to me," said Rachel and she vanished.

"Well, what about the other part," said Greg. "The 'among flowers' bit?"

"The flower shop," said Jackie. "Is there an original wall in there?"

I checked the blueprints and, yes, there was an original wall in the flower shop next door, but how would we get in there and look around without breaking in? I glanced at Jackie and she knew what I was thinking.

"Mel, I don't think that is a good idea."

"What isn't a good idea?" asked Greg.

"We need to get into the flower store next door," I said to him.

"No," Father Hillard said with finality. "I will not be party to breaking the law. Coming here was one thing, since you work here and had the key to get in, but breaking into another store is crossing the line."

He was right, but that hadn't stopped me in the past.

"Hey, Mel!"

We all looked around for the voice, which sounded just like Rachel's.

"Mel, get over here!"

I approached a floor vent. "Rachel?"

"Yeah, it's me," said Rachel. "I found the basement, or cellar, whatever you want to call it."

"How do we get in?"

"That's the tricky part," said Rachel. "There seems to be some loose bricks outside that are covering up a small door. If you all could remove them, you might be able to get in. I'll bang on the door so you can find it."

"Why can't she just show us?" asked Jackie.

"This is Rachel," I replied. "She likes to make a splash."

We all rushed outside to the ally and listened for Rachel's banging. I don't know how she did it, but she hammered the foundation of the building so hard that

I thought she might wake the neighborhood. Greg felt around the brick and found a loose one; the grout had started to decay and crumble from severe weather conditions and normal wear and tear. Greg took out his keys and scraped them against the mortar; it crumbled away in pin-sized pieces before coming off in chunks. A brick popped free. Once he had the one out, it didn't take him long to get the rest until he revealed an old, rotted door with a hooped handle.

Rachel yanked it open. "Surprise!"

"You know, you could have just pushed the bricks free yourself," I said.

"Yeah," replied Rachel with a satisfied grin, "but that wouldn't have been as much fun."

We all pushed our way through the narrow opening and into the cellar, scuffing our feet across the rocky, uneven ground that was nothing more than packed dirt. It hadn't even been covered in floorboards or cement. How long had this been here? And how is it I have been working in the building above it and never knew?

My foot kicked something made of glass. I bent down and picked it up, realizing that it was a chemical used in the development of film. A few abandoned cameras lay scattered across the floor with some pieces of wood leaning against the wall. I guess Gregory had discovered this place and decided to use it as a darkroom. It would work perfectly for developing film.

Brick lined the walls, chipped and grayed from the passage of time, and a small little alcove was nestled deep within the shadows, well away from the small doorway. A draft of air tickled the back of my neck. Looking up, I saw a vent in a piece of ducting that was exposed from a small hole in the ceiling, thus explaining how Rachel had managed to call me. The bottoms of two walls stuck out from the ceiling, hanging about six inches down, but where in the building did they go? Only one person could go into the other stores and investigate: Rachel.

I turned to her. "Rachel, we think that perhaps the wall in flower store might have been hollowed out and used as Gregory's little storage area."

"What?" said Rachel.

Roger stepped forward. "He had a quirk. Gregory always liked to take a few rolls of film from every job and store them someplace for luck. We think that place is in the flower shop."

"Say no more." Rachel disappeared.

I stole a quick glance at Roger and Father Hillard. Roger seemed unphased, but he did speak to Gregory's spirit; Father Hillard seemed calm and interested, despite his reservations about breaking and entering. I think he realized that he had the chance to prove a man's innocence and decided to take it.

"Are you all still down there?" came Rachel's voice through the wall furthest from us.

"Yes!" we all yelled back at her.

"Whew!" said Rachel. "Good. This is the third wall I've yelled down."

Really? I hadn't heard her. There must be some great sound proofing in this building.

"Can you see anything that looks like rolls of film?" I asked.

"No," replied Rachel, "but there seems to be a little space here that could have held something that small. It might have gotten disturbed and fell down the wall."

"Wouldn't the insulation have caught it?" asked Jackie.

"Not necessarily," said Greg. "And some of the other walls didn't have a lot of it anyway."

There was only one way to find out if the film had fallen through the hollow wall and ended up in the cellar. I struck it with the butt of my flashlight. As I tried to hit it again, Father Hillard's hand seized mine, stopping me.

"You're going to hurt yourself," he said and pushed me to the side. He pulled out a pocketknife and stuck the blade in a loose board on the bottom of the wall that I had failed to notice.

"Uh, should you be carrying that?" asked Jackie.

"Pocketknives have their uses. Will you two help me?" Father Hillard pointed at both Greg and Roger.

They each reached up and grabbed the bottom board where Father Hillard had pried it away with his knife and a yanked it free.

Clink. Clink.

Three plastic, cylindrical containers landed on the ground: they were rolls of film. I scooped them up and held them out to Roger. "We need to get these developed and hope that the film hasn't been damaged."

"You're not going anywhere," said a stern voice.

We all whirled around. In our zeal to find the missing film, we never heard the two men behind us sneak inside.

"Edmond Waverly?" said Jackie.

I couldn't believe it either. Though I had a few misgivings about him, he had been more than willing to help me. Donald, Mrs. Waverly's groundskeeper stood next to him. Both held guns pointed at us and neither of them looked happy.

"What is going on here?" demanded Father Hillard.

"The film. Now," said Edmond, ignoring the question.

I clung to the rolls of film, determined not to give them away.

"Why?" asked Roger.

"Roger," spat Edmond. "It's been a while, hasn't it? You knew that I loved Brianna, that I wanted to marry her, but she chose you. She always chose you."

"And you killed her over it?" Jackie was aghast and disgusted.

"You're on these rolls of film, aren't you?" I said, backing away.

"Ah-uh," said Edmond, "no sudden movements."

"Aren't you?" My voice made me sound braver than I felt.

"I knew you would put it together," Edmond said. "From the moment I saw that first article about you, I knew you were dangerous. Only a psychic would have found this place. That was why I had Donald try to kill you, but he hit that cop instead."

A floating board approached Edmond and Donald from behind.

"I was the target?" I couldn't believe it.

"Well, I guess even a psychic can't know everything. The film. Now."

Edmond held his hand out to me.

I tried not to look at the board that hovered in the air and neared him.

"Son," said Father Hillard, "you don't want to do this."

Edmond pointed his gun at him. "Don't tell me what I want to do. You think I won't shoot you? Now give me the film!"

Jackie noticed the approaching board as well. She winked at me.

I reached my hand out, pretending to hand over the rolls of film; but dropped to the ground just as the board smashed into the back of Edmond's head, knocking him over. Jackie dove for another and swung it at Donald, catching him in the stomach, while Rachel struck him in the back. Edmond lunged for me, but Rachel stopped him, throwing him across the room and into the brick wall.

Donald watched as she materialized and his face scrunched up in horror. He ran for the door, but Rachel was upon him in a nanosecond; she seized the collar of his shirt and dragged him to where Edmond slumped on the ground.

"Stay!" she said to him as though he were a dog.

The man's hands shook as he stared at her, unsure of what to do, but frightened of her just the same.

"We need to call the police," said Jackie.

"Taken care of," Rachel said, keeping a watchful eye on both Donald and Edmond.

"How?" asked Jackie.

"It's not that difficult," replied Rachel as though it should have been obvious. "You just pick up the phone and dial."

Sirens sounded and before we knew it, the police barged into the room, yelling at us to throw our hands up. We did. After several moments of confusion, Detective

Henderson and her partner rushed in and told the officers to leave us alone, arresting only Edmond and Donald.

"You imbecile!" Edmond roared are Donald. "You should have killed the witch!"

Rachel smacked him atop the head, though no one saw her.

"Oh yeah," said Detective Henderson, "that's going to play well at your trial." She turned to Roger. "Roger Croukman, unfortunately for you, Mrs. Waverly came forward about an hour ago and confessed everything about the break-ins; and I have to take you in."

"But that's..." started Jackie, but Roger cut her off.

"I did break into the candle store," said Roger.

"Detective"—I handed her the rolls of film—"these are from the night Brianna was murdered. Don't ask me how I know. Just get them developed."

"You know, I could arrest you for impeding a police investigation," said Detective Henderson.

"Over my dead body," snapped Rachel.

Detective Henderson looked all around for the source of the voice, but shrugged her shoulders in the end and ushered us all outside.

Once we had gotten outside into the frigid air—the clouds had cleared and it had finally stopped snowing—I was met by someone I would have preferred to never see again: Jillian Modsen.

"So, Miss Summers," she accosted me, "what led you to this new development? Your ghostly friend?"

"That's it," grumbled Rachel, pulling out a piece of paper with one of Jillian's articles about me. I have no idea how she had gotten it. Before I could do anything,

Rachel had pounced upon Jillian, forced her mouth open, and shoved the crumpled paper into it. People shouted at her to get off and I realized that they actually saw Rachel.

Two officers grabbed her arms and pulled her off Jillian, who coughed and spat up bits of paper.

"I want her arrested for assault," wheezed Jillian.

"Go ahead!" spat Rachel. "And I'm the one who's been vandalizing your car."

I didn't know what to think as I watched Rachel get put into handcuffs, but she winked at me and I knew, at that instant, that she had a plan. An officer placed Rachel in the back of a police cruiser with Jillian hovering nearby, standing next to the car, gloating at having Rachel arrested. As the officer walked to the driver's side, he was stopped by the detective. A devilish grin crossed Rachel's face.

I don't know how she did it; but while the officer was distracted, Rachel jumped out of the vehicle, snapped the cuffs on Jillian's wrists, gagged her, and shoved her into the backseat, shutting the door. The officer finished talking to the detective and got in the car and drove off, never realizing that the switch had been made.

"Have fun!" Rachel called after Jillian and waved.

"Now what?" asked Jackie.

Greg and I looked at each other, but never got a chance to answer her.

"Home," said Father Hillard, coming up to us after giving his statement. "All of you."

None of us argued. We got into our cars and went straight home, where I crawled into bed with my throat feeling as though it had turned into sandpaper.

Chapter 17

Several days had passed since discovering the rolls of film. Detective Shorts had been released from the hospital and informed us that the new evidence would exonerate Roger; and he and Beverly would serve minor sentences for the break-ins, probably no more than six months at most. Jillian had been forced to write a retraction to her articles about me. Her boss was not pleased when he found out that she had spent some time in the back of a police cruiser, and he had gotten a mysterious call from someone threatening a lawsuit.

There was just one more thing to do, but unfortunately I had gotten Tiny's cold. I had managed to get a hold of Tom, despite everything that had gone on, and he had agreed to come over to the apartment.

"So, what's the big surprise?" asked Rachel, appearing in the living room.

Someone knocked at the door. Perfect timing. I opened it, doing my best not to cough and ignore the burning in my throat.

"I'm Tom," said the man, standing before me.

"Come in," I said, trying to disguise my hoarse voice.

He stepped inside, holding his knit hat in his hands. "Look, I don't normally believe in this stuff, but what you said on the phone…"

"Tom?" said Rachel, her usual playful manner had evaporated. She vanished at first, probably unsure of what to do, but reappeared after a few seconds.

Tom seemed unafraid. Perhaps he was just glad to see Rachel again. "Rachel?"

Rachel hugged him as best she could.

I motioned for Jackie and me to leave, giving them their privacy. I don't know how much time had passed, but after a while, I collapsed on my bed, unable to take my sore throat anymore.

"Mel, what's wrong?" asked Jackie.

"My throat hurts," I mumbled into my pillow.

"Oh no! You got Tiny's cold!"

Rachel appeared in my room.

"Rachel," I said, "I thought you would be…"

"We said good-bye," said Rachel, "And I told him to move on. Thanks, Mel, for giving us a chance to say good-bye."

She noticed my weak smile. "What's wrong?"

"She caught Tiny's cold," Jackie answered for me.

"Where's Greg?"

"At work," answered Jackie.

"Don't worry," said Rachel. "I'll take good care of you." She disappeared and reappeared moments later with a carton of chicken soup in her hands. "See? I brought you some soup. Oh, and that five dollars you had in your wallet, it's not there anymore."

"We've got to discuss this whole taking money out of my purse thing," I moaned.

Rachel ignored my last statement as she tucked some blankets around me. "Now you just get all comfy. I'll take good care of you."

That was kind of what I was afraid of.

Get book 11 in the series

Ring Around The Rosy, Not Another Ghosty

About the Author

Janet McNulty currently lives in West Virginia where she continues to work on the Mellow Summers Series. She began the series two years ago as a fluke, but liked writing it so much, that she decided to stick with it.

Besides writing paranormal mysteries, Ms. McNulty has also accomplished success in other genres. She has a fantasy saga (*Legends Lost*) published under the name of Nova Rose and a new dystopian trilogy (*Dystopia*) as well. Ms. McNulty once referred to herself as an author who is "a little something for everyone."

She is currently busy finishing up her science fiction seris (*Solaris Saga*) as well as working on the next Mellow Summers book.

Of course, writing is not the only passion in her life and every author needs some down time. When she isn't working on her books, Ms. McNulty enjoys reading and just poking around in her garden.

More by Janet McNulty

The Mellow Summers Series

Sugar And Spice And Not So Nice
Frogs, Snails, And A Lot Of Wails
An Apple A Day Keeps Murder Away
Three Little Ghosts
Oh Holy Ghost
Where Trouble Roams
Two Ghosts Haunt A Grove
Trick Or Treat Or Murder
Roses Are Red…He's Dead
Double, Double, Nothing But Trouble
Ring Around The Rosy, Not Another Ghosty

Mellow Summers moves to Vermont to attend college, accompanied by her friend Jackie. They soon find themselves running into ghosts and one mystery after another.

The Solaris Saga

Solaris Seethes
Solaris Seeks
Solaris Strays
Solaris Soars

Every myth has a beginning.

After escaping the destruction of her home planet, Lanyr, with the help of the mysterious Solaris, Rynah must put her faith in an ancient legend. Never one to believe in stories and legends, she is forced to follow the ancient tales of her people: tales that also seem to predict her current situation.

Forced to unite with four unlikely heroes from an unknown planet (the philosopher, the warrior, the lover, the inventor) in order to save the Lanyran people, Rynah and Solaris embark on an adventure that will shatter everything Rynah once believed.

The Legends Lost Series

Published under Nova Rose

Tesnayr
Amborese
Galdin

Enter the Lands of Tesnayr and join on an epic fantasy adventure that spans over 1,500 years.

Begin with Tesnayr, the first king of the five lands as he unites the against a savage foe bent on their destruction.

Next, Join Amborese as she fights reclaim the throne after her family was forced to flee from it.

Thinking peace has finally entered the land, follow Galdin as he returns to Tesnayr to find it greatly hanged. Barbarians, led by a mysterious sorcerer, burn and destroy as they go. And only Galdin can stop them if he chooses to accept his fate.

Visit www.legendslosttrilogy.com to learn more about the Legends Lost Trilogy.

The Dystopia Trilogy

Dystopia (Book 1)
Tempered Steel (Book 2)
Liberty's Torch (Book 3)

**Imagine living in a world where
everything you do is controlled.**

Dana Ginary lives in a world where every aspect of her life is controlled by the Dystopian Government. Forced to work in Waste Management, her life becomes a nightmare with hunger and survival is her only constant. Before she knows it, she is caught up in a resistance movement and exiled from Dystopia, forced to find her way in the barren wastelands. While there, she must learn to live independently and discover how far she is willing to go to live and achieve freedom.

Grandpa's Stories

My grandfather grew up in Arizona during the 1920s and 1930s. One week after the attack on Pearl Harbor he joined the Navy. During the summer of 2012, my mother visited him and recorded his stories about growing up, World War II, and his time as an employee at the Pacific Bell Telephone Company. This is the history of the 20th century as he lived it. These recordings make up this book. These are his words.